D0465133

AN UNINTERRUPTED VIEW
OF THE SKY

Also by Melanie Crowder

Audacity

AN
UNINTERRUPTED
VIEW
OF THE
SKY

MELANIE CROWDER

PHILOMEL BOOKS

PHILOMEL BOOKS
an imprint of Penguin Random House LLC
375 Hudson Street
New York, NY 10014

Copyright © 2017 by Melanie Crowder.
Penguin supports copyright. Copyright fuels creativity, encourages diverse voices, promotes free speech, and creates a vibrant culture. Thank you for buying an authorized edition of this book and for complying with copyright laws by not reproducing, scanning, or distributing any part of it in any form without permission. You are supporting writers and allowing Penguin to continue to publish books for every reader.

Philomel Books is a registered trademark of Penguin Random House LLC.

Library of Congress Cataloging-in-Publication Data is available upon request.

Printed in the United States of America.
ISBN 9780399169007
10 9 8 7 6 5 4 3 2 1
Edited by Liza Kaplan.
Design by Ellice M. Lee.
Text set in Garamond.
Barbed wire art © sharpner/Shutterstock.
This is a work of fiction. Names, characters, places, and incidents either are the product of the author's imagination or are used fictitiously, and any resemblance to actual persons, living or dead, businesses, companies, events, or locales is entirely coincidental.

In Memory of

MICHELLE BEGLEY AND
DRA. WENDY LAGRAVA ZAMORANO

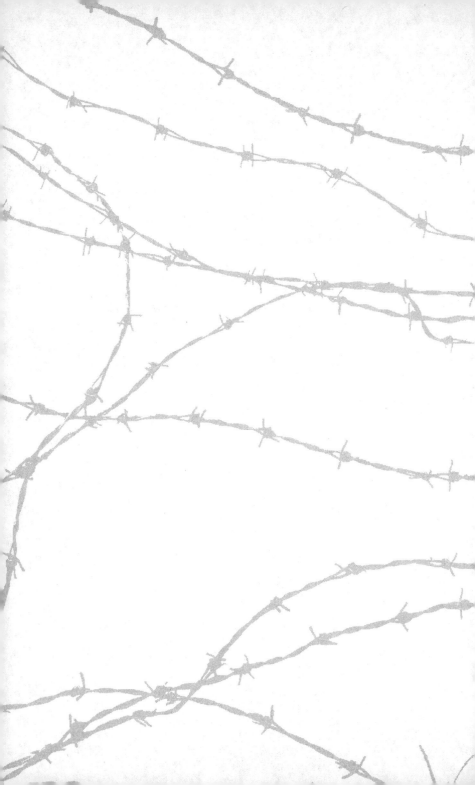

COCHABAMBA, BOLIVIA

1999

October 6

t's just a bare rectangle of dirt, maybe half the size of a real field. No lines, no goals, and not even one blade of grass. But it's where Reynaldo and the guys and I go the second the noon bell rings and we're free. We peel off our school uniforms, trade our dress shoes for cleats, and start knocking the ball around as we divvy up, shirts and skins. I'm almost always the shortest one out there, but I'm quick and my feet are liquid on the ball.

Five minutes in, and whatever has been going wrong that day slips through your fingers like the string that tethers a balloon to the ground. It's just gone.

Ten minutes in, and sweat sticks my jersey down the bumpy ridge of my spine. Our forearms slide against one another, elbowing and jamming our bodies into position. Our feet kick up the dust, and the ball bounces through a cloud of knees and bare shins and curses and jeers.

It starts out friendly enough, just some guys from school, and a few from the neighborhood who dropped out years ago. But street games like this take on a pulse of their own, and sometimes guys we don't know get drawn in. They take sides, and the game shifts. The jeers quiet and the laughter stops. It's one thing to play against your friends, when it's all just for fun, and in worship of the almighty fútbol.

But when new players step on, all of a sudden everybody has something to prove. And when the new guys look like this—sporting the new season's jerseys and cleats we've only ever seen in catalogs, and skin so white they don't even look mestizo—I know it's going to be bad for me.

I've come to expect it by now—cleats-up tackles, hip checks to knock me off the ball, and a few too many shoves from behind. It's not just me that gets it. They go after Mauricio, too, who's darker than the rest, and shorter, who looks just like his indigenous Quechua parents.

Honest—I don't go looking for fights. It's just, they always seem to be looking for me.

I'm two steps from the goal when an elbow cracks against my eyebrow. Blood slicks down my cheek and drips onto the dirt in front of me.

That's it. The game is over and I'm in their faces and my fists are up and—

"Hey!" Reynaldo yells as he hauls me back from the tangle of cussing, blustering guys that's one punch away from an all-out brawl. "Hey! Francisco! Forget those bastards." I hardly hear him, even though he's shouting in my face. He holds me back and ducks his head so I have to look him in the eyes. It works.

I leave the field and that fight behind me.

Reynaldo and I sling our backpacks over our shoulders and start walking home. The sun is high overhead. The blood dries on my cheek and cracks into flakes that fall away from my skin.

We don't talk about what happened back there. What's there to say? All people see when they look at me is my dark skin and my Aymara face, no matter how I dress or talk or how bad I can kick their ass on the fútbol field.

What good does it do to talk about it?

Reynaldo and I weave through the dusty streets of our neighborhood. It's better than some, I guess. But not so good that when Mamá goes out with her work friends, she brings them here. No, they go to a restaurant, or to someone else's house in a better part of Cochabamba, with manicured gardens and trash collection and sidewalks.

The stores over there are shinier, the cars sleeker, and don't think I don't notice—everybody's skin is lighter, too. Mamá and my little sister, Pilar, with their pale skin and delicate features, might have a chance at brushing shoulders with the elite, but not me.

It's just the way it is.

Light-skinned mestizos work in the banks and the architect offices and the government buildings. Dark-skinned Aymaras and Quechuas work in the cancha and the fields and the mines. And then there's me, stuck somewhere in between.

I'm not a peasant like my grandparents. I'm not a dreamer like Papá. So what if I am hiding my dark skin and my campesino roots under modern clothes and ready fists? What's so wrong with that?

I know the streets of this neighborhood. I know where I belong. So I'll set up shop with Reynaldo, and I'll play fútbol every day, and nobody will ever expect anything more from me.

The whole walk home, Reynaldo tries to distract me, talking about a wholesaler from La Paz who will sell us last season's jerseys cheap, so we can start small with a stall at the big market in town, the cancha. He says if we take whatever work we can find after we graduate in six weeks, we might get our stall up and running by the spring.

Six more weeks, and then my life is finally my own.

Pilar is already home when I get there. She's sitting on the couch with the entire contents of her backpack spilled out around her. The house smells like the dough that's rising under a towel in the kitchen. The light is soft; Mamá has this thing with lamps. There are, like, seven in every room.

It takes a minute for Pilar to notice me. "What happened to your face?"

"Nothing."

"It looks gross."

"Thanks." I swipe a roll off the counter. "I'm going to take a shower. Did Mamá call?"

"She says she'll be home at six, and that you have to do your homework."

"Yeah, yeah."

At the end of the hall, I turn into my room and brush aside the sheet tacked across the middle to make it seem like Pilar and I each have our own private space.

We don't.

To prove it, before I can throw a towel over my shoulder and leave again, Pilar is there, standing at the border between her half of the room and mine.

"Guess what?" she says. "Maria went to La Paz with her family last weekend."

I don't answer. Sometimes if I ignore her, she gives up and leaves me alone.

"Have you ever been to La Paz?"

"Once." It's more like a grunt than an actual word.

"What was it like? Is it big? The people there are Aymara, mostly, like Abuelo and Abuela, right? Not like the Quechua Cochabambinos." She barely breaks for a breath. "Do they really build their houses on the sides of the mountains?"

It wasn't a big deal, sharing a room when she was three and I was twelve. But now she's eight and I'm seventeen. A bedsheet is not privacy. Not even close.

Lucky for me, tonight Mamá and Papá are too busy arguing to notice the cut over my eye. They've been doing this a lot lately—fighting about money. Pilar and I take our plates into our room and eat there.

I mean, I get it. Mamá hates being reminded every day that we're barely scraping by.

Papá hates that everything he's worked his whole life to achieve still isn't enough for her.

October 7

The thing about Mamá is she never stays mad long. She gets mad quick, but she melts quick too. Papá says it's all that Spanish heat burning up her veins. I've got the same temper, but nobody looks at me and sees a drop of European blood. Hence the cut on my eyebrow that swelled to the size of an egg overnight.

This morning, since they've clearly made up, my parents are free to gang up on me. As usual, Papá is all earnest and rational, and Mamá—I never know if she's going to swat me with a dish towel for my smart mouth or smash my cheeks between her palms and cover my face with kisses. Just now, I'd rather the swat. My face is killing me.

Papá is on me because I didn't finish my history home-work last night. And then there's the black eye. Pilar sits across from us at the table, her legs swinging back and forth beneath her chair. She's eating her pan con queso in small, measured bites while her eyes dart between Papá and me and Mamá, who's leaning against the kitchen counter, her mug of coffee raised to her lips so the steam bathes her cheeks.

"You need to take your schoolwork seriously," Papá says. "Learning is a privilege."

"Oh, yeah? You sit through one week of Profesor Muñoz's algebra class and then tell me you still think so."

Snap. Ow. "Listen to your father."

"Francisco, the only thing holding you back is your own lack of initiative."

"Really, Papá? That's the only thing?"

He sighs and tries another angle. "Francisco, history is not just academic. An understanding of where we've come from as a country will help you understand where we are going, and how you can be a part of that."

"I don't need to pay attention in history class to open a shop with Reynaldo."

"Working a stall in the cancha to sell cleats and jerseys is not ambition."

"Come on, Papá."

"You are more than this."

"So I can't do what I want with my life—I have to live the life you wish you'd had?"

I get a look for that one. "My son, I want you to have a good life. I want you to not always be scraping by. If you go to university—"

I can't listen to any more of this. I push back from the table, sling my backpack over my shoulder.

"If you could get a degree like your mother—"

I leave, letting the door slam behind me.

When is he going to get it? All this opportunity he thinks he missed—it doesn't exist. It was never there, not for someone who looks like me.

I don't think there's anything I hate more than disappointing Papá. So I finish my history homework in math class, which means I'll have to figure out whatever Profesor Muñoz was droning on about in algebra after school.

Or not.

Nobody needs this stuff in real life, do they? But then I'd fail the test on Friday and get that look from Papá again.

And I'd be right back where I started.

After school, we've barely started our game when Mamá shows up at the field, out of breath and red-faced. Did she run all the way here? Mamá never runs, anywhere, for any reason. She didn't even take off those clunky high-heeled shoes, or unbutton the blazer that cinches like a straitjacket over her ribs all day at the bank.

Wait—why isn't she at work?

"Francisco!" Mamá calls. "You need to come home. Right now."

I kick the ground, and a cloud of dirt swirls around my shins. "Our game's not over."

"We have to go. Now."

"Ay, Má!"

"*Francisco!*" She's gasping for breath. Her hair is sliding out of its clip. My mother's always-busy hands hang at her sides, between the folds of her skirt like a pair of felled doves.

It's all wrong.

So I go, and the guys chuck me on the shoulder as I leave the game.

I think about spinning around and cracking the ball through the posts, clenching my fists and shouting GOOOOOOOOOOOOOOOOOOOOOAL as I back away. But I don't. I trail behind Mamá. Now that I'm not running anymore, I can smell myself. I need a shower.

"What's going on, Mamá?"

Her lips stay glued together like slabs of dough pinched and sealed at the edges. I don't get a word out of her the whole way home.

We swing through the iron gate set into the brick wall that wraps around our house, and step across the stone path to the door. Mamá's begonias look thirsty. And I guess it's time to empty the ashes from the trash pit at the back of the yard. Did she call me home to do chores?

I duck my head to pass under the wooden beam and keep it down, as I always do inside our house, the soft light and the low ceiling hanging over me like an unresolved argument. Mamá closes the door behind us.

Pilar is standing in the middle of the kitchen, like she's been waiting in that spot all afternoon for us to walk in. "Mamá, what's wrong?" Pilar asks.

Mamá doesn't turn around to face us.

"Papá ran out of gas on the highway." Her words are muffled.

I don't get it. "What do you want me to do about it? I don't have a car. I guess I could ask Reynaldo's mother to drive me, but—"

"Francisco!" Mamá spins to face me then, slamming her hand against the kitchen table. "No interruptions."

Pilar backs into the space between the counter and the oven. Her backpack slides to the floor, and for once, she has nothing to say. My sister hates it when we yell. She and Papá— they're the gentle ones. Mamá and I are the hotheads, too alike not to fight.

"Your father picked up a customer this morning who needed to go far out of the city. Papá didn't think he had enough gas, but the man was impatient, and it was a big fare." Her shoulders lift and fall again in a shrug, and she brushes a row of crumbs from the counter into her bare palm. "We need the money. So he took it.

"Your father dropped the customer off and turned back to Cochabamba, but the tank went empty a few kilometers from the gas station. He had to walk along the highway the whole way there and back. But he never made it to the taxi. The police stopped him and arrested him, said that he was going to make cocaine with that gasoline."

Mamá leans over the sink. Her head hangs below her shoulders, and her fingers grip the chipped porcelain. "It's a lie, and they know it."

I lick my lips and try to swallow, but my voice still cracks when I speak. "Arrested? The police have Papá?"

With a sigh, Mamá shrugs out of her blazer, and the sharp

angles of shoulder pads and lapels slump onto the counter. "Your father is in prison."

She kicks off her shoes and reaches out to Pilar. My sister's feet skim silently across the floor, and she buries her face between Mamá's belly and the fleshy inside of her arm.

"He was in the wrong place at the wrong time, it's as simple as that. He has rights, like every other citizen of this country, but somehow the drug law that they got your father on is outside of that. I've never heard of a single person who got out after being arrested because of the one thousand eight."

Pilar's shoulders start to shake.

"So what—the 1008 is a drug law?" I sputter. "Papá doesn't have anything to do with drugs. Mamá, I don't understand."

"Your father didn't do anything wrong." Mamá rubs Pilar's back. She sighs again. "Not that being innocent makes any difference."

The brick walls of our house are always bouncing sound back and forth, little scrapes and whispered words echoing on themselves so that it's never really quiet inside. But right now, the walls have nothing to say.

"What do you mean?" I ask. "If he's innocent, we'll get him out."

"Francisco, we spent our entire savings to buy your father's taxi last year. We can't afford a lawyer, or the court fees, or the bribes needed to put his case in front of a judge. We barely make the rent each month, and that's with both my income and your father's. Without his?" She draws a hand over her mouth like she's wiping away words she doesn't want to say, but that she can't seem to hold in. "It's impossible."

"I can drive the taxi, Mamá. I'll take over Papá's work and help us make the rent."

It's not like I need a reason to leave school. If Papá would have allowed it, I would have quit years ago. Maybe if I'd been working all this time, he could have passed up that fare.

Mamá shakes her head. "The taxi was impounded. Confiscated by the police as evidence."

"Evidence of what? Papá's not driving cocaine around in his taxi all day. That is ridiculous!"

Mamá's angry too, that this happened to Papá. I can see it in the clicking of her jaw, in her hand whipping into the air and down again. But, more than anything, I think maybe Mamá is mad at Papá.

The sun sets, and the sky begins to yellow at the edges. Mamá pulls the pot filled with leftovers from last night's sopa de maní out of the refrigerator and sets it on the stove. Pilar moves a stool in front of the cupboards and lifts down four bowls and four cups. Then she looks at the dishes in her hands and slowly puts one set back. Her shoulders hitch, and her eyes slide toward Mamá. They're big and brown and just . . . sad.

There are only three of us tonight.

I leave the kitchen for my parents' room. Papá's still there, all the little pieces of him. The sheets where he slept last night are pooled in little circles where his hips and shoulders rested. A glass of dusty water waits by the bed, the imprint of his lips on the rim like the mark on a communion cup before the priest wipes it away. Papá's notebook lies open, the lined page indented with the ghost letters of the last poem he wrote. I run my fingers over the ragged edges of ripped-out pages.

I walked out on him this morning. He was trying to tell me something, and I just walked out. Heat rushes up through my bones and flexes my fingertips. My brain hasn't even begun to catch up, but my feet are set and my right shoulder cocks back and—*BAM*. My fist slams into the side of the bookcase. And then my left, and my right again.

The bookcase is solid wood. It doesn't split, but the skin over my knuckles does. Pilar rushes into the doorway, and the lace curtains at the window throw veined shadows over her face. A drop of sweat slides into my eyes, and I blink the sting away. My chest heaves with angry breath.

"Francisco?"

"Just leave me alone."

I back away, cradling my throbbing hand against my stomach, and head to my bedroom.

I brush the sheet aside and fall into bed. I stare at the ceiling, too many thoughts fighting with one another for space in my head. My hand is on fire. The inside of my skull is noise.

I shake my head to clear it, and a flash of white catches my eye: a folded square of paper tucked under the lamp base.

I reach with my not-busted hand and pry the paper out from its hiding spot. It crackles as I unbend the folds one by one—looks like it's been that way for a while. I smooth the page open. Narrow stanzas spill down the creased page.

My hands begin to shake.

My father is a poet. He was born and raised in a small Andean community on the high plains, the Altiplano, which stretches between the Cordilleras twelve thousand feet above sea level. The Altiplano is huge—too big to be contained by the boundaries of any one country. There are a few cities up there, but in the space between them, it's all thousand-year-old ruins and tiny settlements and empty swaths of rugged, untouched land.

Maybe if Papá had grown up someplace like Oruro or Potosí, that had electricity and running water and good schools, it would have been different. Instead, he grew up in an isolated community that had watched the rise and fall of the Inka and of the Spaniards, and though they were driven to the ground again and again, held to their ways as the world shifted around them.

There was only a simple school where my father grew up. They taught whoever showed up how to read and write in Spanish, the language of the conquistadors. Papá got in only two years of school. There's no time for study when you have to work the fields so you can eat.

But the words he learned there stayed with him long after he left for the busy city below. Maybe it was the thin air of his childhood that made my father hear symphonies in paper napkins tumbling down the road, that made him see mosaics in the flutter of pigeon wings lifting from the plaza stones. Or maybe it was just who he was all along.

Every day, for the past twelve years, while Papá drove a taxi from one end of Cochabamba to the other, he arranged words in his mind, scribbling down a phrase or two in between fares. At night, he'd tuck the finished poem—a folded piece of paper—into my shoe, or Mamá's hair, or the coat pocket of Pilar's doll.

This was one of those. Maybe my father's last poem for me.

For My Eagle, My Francisco

The rooster struts on the roofline of his hutch, his palace,
Master of all he surveys,
His beak, with each step, stabbing the air
As if to say, You—
I will cut you
And you
And you—

How exhausting to be on attack all day!

The eagle does not strut
He does not fluff his feathers
Or preen or scream,
Rake his talons across the winds
That dare to sniff out his lofty nest.
He is still
He is calm, assured
Master of himself.

Papá thinks if I just reach for this better version of myself, my life could be some noble thing. But he didn't grow up in this city. He doesn't know what it's like. He doesn't realize that a scrappy rooster is the best I'll ever be.

Mamá doesn't sit down once all night. She scours the house for soap and combs and towels and clothes, and shoves things into boxes, filling the trunk that has been in her family for eight generations. Since General Ballivián, she always says.

She continues to work long after Pilar goes to sleep. I lie down, too, but I'm just throwing my weight back and forth on the creaky springs, unable to sleep without the low rumble of Papá's voice in the other room, and the buzz and breath of his snores.

All night, I hear the sound of clinking glasses, the muffled thuds of heavy things bumping against one another, as though the bones of the world I have lived in my whole life are breaking and being knit back together at odd angles, against their will.

October 8

Pilar and I skip school, Mamá calls in sick to work, and we walk together to the bus stop. We climb on and squeeze into the space between bench seats. Mamá's carrying a bag over her shoulder with a few things for Papá, and she presses Pilar to her side.

The chatter and clatter of people crammed together elbows me from all around. I hold Papá's notebook against my chest. The skin on my bruised and split knuckles stretches, and I loosen my grip. My eyes find the window. Only a scrap of blue is visible above the maze of dusty brick walls.

We get off, walk the last few blocks, and stand in the plaza opposite the men's prison. Stark letters frame the entrance: CÁRCEL SAN SEBASTIÁN. Cars whizz by, honking and swerving. People saunter through the plaza, unaware of what's going on behind that cracked yellow stucco. Then again, maybe they know and they just don't care.

This part of the street is blocked off, and—who knows why—filled with wooden bed frames. We could cross, but we don't. Pilar grabs Mamá's hand as her eyes travel up to the high, narrow windows, to the row of shacks—cells, I guess—balanced like birdhouses on the roof. Two guards stand on the upper wall with guns on their backs, watching everything below.

"It will be noisy in there, and crowded," Mamá says. "It's not like those gringo TV shows you watch at Reynaldo's house—with concrete walls and floors, and cells with bars and electronic locks and prisoners in jumpsuits. This will be very different."

Mamá keeps shifting her weight to one foot and then the other, almost taking a step forward and then pulling back again at the last minute.

She runs a hand across her mouth. "It's over, once you end up in there."

"What is?" Pilar asks. "What's over?"

But Mamá doesn't answer. Shadows from the palm trees above cut across her forehead and the bridge of her nose. I can't see her eyes.

"He'll be waiting for us. We can't stand here all day," she says, but it's like she's convincing herself more than anything.

We cross together, pass through a set of carved wooden doors and into a dark entryway. The only thing between us and the prison is a metal gate. Mamá stops to sign in with guards in green uniforms holding rifles across their chests. They're not only guards. They're policemen. Just like the ones who arrested Papá.

Bastards.

With a *clank* and a sliding chain, we're in.

I don't know what I thought a men's prison would look like. But not this. The center of the place is a courtyard packed with people—men talk in groups and play cards and carve little wooden toys. It's loud. And really crowded.

There are no guards inside, only prisoners.

Plastic tables bake in the sun, and a basketball hoop without a net hangs from one of the balconies. On all four sides of the courtyard are stalls and little stores that sell toilet paper and toothpaste, or picante de pollo with chuño. In the empty spaces, mattresses are propped up against the walls.

A voice crackles over the intercom, calling a prisoner to the guard station. The sounds of saws and hammers echo out of the hallways that peel away from the center of the prison. All around us are cells. Some of them are so small you have to crawl to get inside. Or they're stacked on top of each other and you have to climb a rickety ladder to get in. Some are just pieced-together slabs of junk that look like a tower of cardboard boxes.

Is that where Papá slept last night—in one of those?

It's noisy. It's dirty. My skin itches. My lungs close. How can Papá be here? How can my gentle papá belong in this place?

And then I see him—dressed in the same clothes as yesterday, only rumpled, his face smeared with dirt. The skin under his eyes is heavy and dark. He waves a far-off wave, like even though he's only a few steps away, we'll never be able to reach him. He smiles, but it isn't a smile I recognize. That isn't *him*.

"Papá!" Pilar drops Mamá's hand and runs to him. She wraps her arms around his waist and stares up into his face. "I want you to come home."

"I want that too, so much, *wawitay*. But I have to stay here for now."

Pilar's arms loosen, and she turns her face to the side, resting it against his stomach. "But why?"

Papá pries Pilar's arms away and kneels in front of her. "I have to stay here until I can prove that I didn't do anything wrong."

She blinks at the dark hallways sliding one into another, the milling crowd of haggard men, the dangling electrical wires hanging like jungle vines from the walls. "Where will you sleep?"

"I'll get a cell soon," he says. "As soon as I can pay for one. No lazybones here." He wiggles Pilar's shoulders side to side. She always laughs when he does that, but it doesn't work this time.

"You have to pay for your cell?"

Mamá slaps my arm. Okay—I guess I deserved that. I should have said something else, like *hello* or *are you okay?*

"Yes, if I want to sleep in a cell I have to rent the space. Don't worry, Francisco. As soon as I have a chance to explain, I'm sure they will let me go."

I hold out Papá's notebook and pen. He takes them and closes his arms over the creased binding.

"Thank you, my son." He stands and places his hand

against the back of my neck, warm and steady. How can he still be so steady in here?

I should say something to make him feel better. I should feel something besides my own fear. But I swear, those walls are closing in on me. Like if I let that prison gate close behind me, I'll never get out again.

Pilar and I sit on the stone steps in the prison courtyard with Mamá and Papá, staring at nothing and everything. Something is up with my parents. I don't think she's raised her eyes above his chin all day.

And she doesn't touch anything. Mamá perches on the edge of the step, her arms crossed and her knees pressed together, like if she keeps to herself, this place can't get to her.

We don't talk. What more do we have to say to one another? So I watch the sun move behind the clouds. The high walls and fluttering laundry crop the edges of the sky into a jagged square—you can't see where the blue meets the ragged brown of the hills surrounding the city.

Even in the open courtyard, it's oppressive.

Sometime after noon, the gates open and a dozen kids—some I recognize from school, others even younger than Pilar—file into the prison, their white uniforms coated with a layer of orange dust from the streets outside. Once they're in, they disappear into the back of the prison or tramp up the stairwell to the upper levels, where cells rim the balcony overlooking the courtyard below.

One of the guys from school stops and looks me over. José, I think. No one Reynaldo and I would hang out with. Not because he's younger than us, but because he always looks like he rolled in a trash heap before coming to school. I guess now I know why.

José's eyebrows raise in a question, and I want to knock

it right off his face. *No, I am* not *just like you. I am not anything like you.*

"Do those kids live here?" Pilar asks.

"Yes," Papá says. "If they have no other place to go, the whole family moves into the prison."

We watch as half of the kids leave again, their school uniforms traded for street clothes, their arms filled with trays of wooden toys or food to sell outside. Anything that will help their families pay for life in here.

Mamá goes back through the gate to the guard station in the entryway of the prison to ask about visiting hours, and meals, and notes from the outside coming and going. Papá takes us to see the wood shop where the prisoners make furniture to be sold in the plaza across the street. The beds they make support the families that live with them in prison, or the ones who can afford to live outside the walls.

"I can quit school and help pay the rent," I say to Papá. "I can get a job until they let you out. I can take care of Mamá and Pilar, and you, too."

"No, Francisco. You think because I am in prison, that means my plans for you have changed? You think I will give up on you so easily?"

The hours pass slowly. I leave Pilar with Papá and go looking for the bathroom at the back of the prison. The smell lets me know when I'm close. Inside, there's a rusted metal sink in the corner where one of the prisoners is scrubbing sharp-smelling soap into a bucket full of clothes. He cuts his eyes to me as I step inside.

"I wouldn't go in there. Toilet's backed up again."

And that's when I notice the floor. The drain in the middle of the concrete can't keep up with the water and . . . other stuff flowing out of the toilet. I pick up my feet—the soles of my shoes are slick with it. My throat seizes, and I back out of there, a hand over my mouth to keep from retching.

Never mind, I don't have to go.

My eyes water as I make it into the hallway. I'm not looking where I'm going, and I almost run into two guys pinning another prisoner against the wall. One of them has a knife. All three of them are staring at me now.

I can hold my own in a fistfight with other guys my age, but this? I'm not cut out for this. I back away and break into a run. What was Mamá thinking, bringing us here? And how is Papá ever going to survive this place?

When I get back to the courtyard, I slow my run to a walk. The last of the kids are back, spilling in and out of shadowed doorways. Most of them disappear into cells, the doors clicking one after another and locking them inside. Yeah. I'd lock the door too if I had to live here.

The stream of people coming in and out of the prison gate slows to a stop.

"You two should get going now." Papá stands and wipes off his hands. "I wonder what's taking your mother so long?"

There's a catch in his voice. Papá's shoulders are slumped,

and his head droops low. I look away as he turns and walks over to the gate between us and the guard station, where Mamá passed through a while ago.

"Come on, Pilar." I tap her on the shoulder. "It's time to—"

"My wife did *what?*" Papá yells.

Pilar and I run over to the gate. Papá's eyes are wide, his hands clamped against the sides of his head.

"Papá?" Pilar whispers.

He lowers his hands, and pulls us close.

The guard on the other side of the gate looks bored. He shrugs his shoulders. "She left. About thirty minutes ago."

Papá blinks, like he's trying to catch his mind up to the things he's hearing. "What if something happened to her? What if she's—"

"No. I was right here. She signed out and just walked away."

"But the children—she didn't take Francisco and Pilar. Why wouldn't she take our children with her?"

"Maybe she didn't realize we lock the gate at six," the guard says, "and she'll be back later tonight."

Pilar tugs Papá's hand. "Maybe she went out to get us dinner."

Papá pats Pilar's hand, but he doesn't take his eyes off the guard. I don't either. Something about the way the guy said that last part wasn't right. Like he didn't believe his own words.

"The truth, please," Papá says softly.

The guard twists the barrel of the rifle in his hands. "It happens sometimes. A man ends up in here and . . . it's all too much—too hard to raise the kids alone on the outside. The wife leaves." The guard shrugs again. "It doesn't happen often. But sometimes."

Now he looks guilty? Now?

"Look, the kids can stay here with you until the boy turns eighteen. Then just the girl."

"Here?" I think Papá has stopped breathing altogether. "My children, living here?"

"The prison director prefers they be transferred to an orphanage, but those facilities are currently above capacity—"

"My children are not orphans!"

The guard holds up a hand, and Papá takes a step back.

"It is best if they can stay with family outside the prison. But if there is no one who will take them, then yes, your children can live here with you."

I can't feel my fingers. I can't feel my legs. "Let me go," I say to Papá. "Let me go find her—it must have been a mistake. She wouldn't just leave us here! Let me talk to her."

"You can't," the guard says with another shrug. "The gate is locked for the night. No one leaves again until morning."

Papá stretches his arm across my chest to hold me back. Pilar's head is bobbing up and down as her breath comes out in raspy gasps.

I thought Mamá was just angry. I thought she didn't stay with us and try to comfort Papá because she was worried about the money and how she was going to take care of us all by herself. I thought last night Mamá was packing things for Papá, so his time at the prison wouldn't be so hard, and so he could have a little of home with him here.

Seventeen. Almost a man. How can I still be so stupid?

"I'll go get her in the morning, Papá. I'll bring her back."

The words are slow to leave him. "If it makes you feel better, Francisco, go to the house and look for her tomorrow. But I think if your mother could leave you in this place for even one night, then she is gone. There's no one left for you to find."

The sun dips below the prison walls. Two guards come inside, and a voice crackles over the intercom. Papá nudges us back against the interior prison wall, and he walks to the middle of the courtyard. Above and all around us, doors open, and feet shuffle across the concrete and down the ladders and stairwells from the upper levels.

Men flood out of the hallways and into the courtyard until they are lined up in tightly packed rows. They keep coming until the courtyard is full, their bodies blocking what little light is left in the sky. I don't know what's worse, the noise or the stink. I pull the corner of my shirt over my nose. Pilar claps her hands over her ears and sidles behind me. Her whole body trembles.

Papá's eyes meet mine, and what I see there rips open something inside me. He's not hard enough to survive this place. Neither is my sister.

After about twenty minutes, the guards seem satisfied and they leave, locking the gate behind them. The prisoners head back to their cells or begin claiming pieces of the ground on the balconies or between the railing and the doors to the cells for the prisoners who can pay. Beneath the stairs is best, or under a table in the courtyard so no one will step on you in the middle of the night. Some have a blanket to roll up in, or a mattress; others, like us, have nothing but the clothes they're wearing.

Before all the space along the wall is taken, Papá pulls us into a corner. He puts Pilar against the wall, with his body and mine between her and the rest of the men.

A prisoner goes around to everyone planning to sleep on the ground and collects a boliviano from each one. Papá digs in his pocket and hands it over, like he's not even surprised that we have to pay to sleep on the concrete. How much more money does he have? And what happens if he runs out? What more can they do to us?

Soon, the day sounds of the prison fade and the night sounds take over: snores, bodies shifting on the ground, insects rubbing their serrated wings together.

I lie on my back in between Pilar and Papá, our shoulders staggered so the three of us fit in the tight space. My eyelids become heavy, but they don't close. They don't even blink as the sky turns from blue to gray to suffocating black.

October 9

I n the morning, we peel ourselves off the concrete and dust the worst of the dirt from our clothes. My eyelids are like sandpaper, and my mouth is gritty, as if I rolled in the stuff all night long. I can't turn my head to the side without the muscles in my neck and shoulders locking up.

The front gate to the prison opens with a groan, and I jump to my feet. Papá catches my wrist. "We will figure this out, Francisco."

"She's there. She has to be."

"Okay." It's obvious he's just saying that. He doesn't believe it. "But if she isn't, you can't stay in our house. The rent is due in a couple of days, and if we don't pay, someone else will move in. I don't want you there when the landlord comes."

He releases my hand. "I can start work Monday in the wood shop. You and Pilar will go to school, just like always. I'll save up for rent and get us a cell as soon as I can."

"Yeah, okay," I mumble and start to walk toward the gate. Pilar runs after me.

"I want to come with you."

"No way."

"She's my mother too!"

I can hear it in her voice—everything that's churning inside me, ready to spill over. But I can't. I can't deal with her heartbreak and mine too. "You'll only get in the way. Stay here with Papá."

I retrace yesterday's steps back to the bus stop. On board, I wrap an arm around the metal bar and shove both hands in my pockets to keep myself upright. Mothers with their hands full and shuffling abuelos smile at me as if I'm doing some great chivalrous thing, not taking a seat.

But I'm not trying to be polite. My body is a skeleton, clattering around with nothing to hold it together. If I sit down, I might not get back up again. If I don't keep moving, I might tumble to the ground, just a pile of bones.

I ride the bus home, if I can call it that anymore.

I don't even remember getting off and walking three streets over to the house. One minute I'm on the bus, and the next I'm standing in the shade of our scraggly jacaranda tree, my fingers curled through the bars of the iron gate.

I want to know if she's really gone—I have to know. But I don't go right in. If I can live a few more seconds with maybe, I will.

I take a breath, or three, then I lift the latch, push through, and walk across the stones to the front of the house. I turn the handle and the door to the kitchen swings wide. The cupboards are bare and hanging open. The lace that used to cover the kitchen table is gone, and a sun-bleached web patterns the wood where it used to lie.

The bed and dresser are still there in my parents' bedroom, but the life is gone from the place. Everything that was *them* is gone. I walk down the hall and into the room I shared with Pilar. Before last night, I had no idea how fortunate we were to have a house with walls between us and the rest of the city. And a bedroom just for Pilar and me to share? A palace.

In the living room, three boxes wait on the carpet. Mamá's handwriting scrawls across the cardboard: *Papá, Pilar, Francisco.* One for each of us. I lift the lid off mine. Soap. A comb. Clothes. A towel. Some books for school. The *chu'lo* Papá knitted for me when I was little and a leaning stack of the poems he's written for me over the years.

There is nothing from Mamá. No note. No explanation.

It's like a tackle from behind that you don't see coming, that sends you crashing to the ground and knocks the breath from your lungs. And you somehow get up onto your hands and knees, and you gasp and you gasp and you gasp, but it doesn't seem like any air will make it past your throat ever again.

I drift into the kitchen. She probably went to her parents' house in La Paz, to the grandparents I've never met, who don't approve of her *indio* husband and the children they had together.

I could go after her. I could make her come back. But the thought sweeps out of my head just as quickly. She doesn't want us. So what's the point?

Besides, there must be a thousand Vargases in La Paz. It's no good. I kick the cupboard below the sink shut. It bangs against the wood frame and flies back open. So I kick it again. And again. And again. And again. The sound splits the air in the kitchen, and even after the house has gone silent, the noise echoes against my eardrums.

Breathing hard and limping a little, I lean down and close the cupboard door with my fingertips. It hangs off the hinge, a split tearing through the wood grain.

Just outside the door, I notice a wheelbarrow propped against the side of the house. Mamá knew I wouldn't be able to carry all this back to the prison without help. A laugh scrapes past my throat. She thought of everything. Everything she needed to clear the way so her conscience would let her leave us behind.

stack the boxes on the wheelbarrow and push it outside. Where am I supposed to put all this? Like Papá said, if we don't make the payments, someone else will move into this house and then all our things will be thrown into the fire pit. We don't have a cell at the prison, so it's no use lugging the stuff there.

I close the door behind me. It isn't our house anymore. I'm not sure why I bother. But something won't let me leave the door open, let dust and litter and bugs claim it so quickly.

I push the wheelbarrow over the ruts in the dirt road, a few blocks down, to Reynaldo's. I ring the bell, and his mother answers. When she sees me at the gate, her hands start flapping like wet laundry in the wind—slapping against her cheeks, touching the rosary around her neck, and patting my shoulders. I set the wheelbarrow down with a *clunk* and follow her into the house.

Yeah, everybody's heard about it. Everybody's *so* sorry.

She walks with me down the hall to Reynaldo's room. He's lucky—he got his own bedroom after his older brothers moved out.

I knock and let myself in. Reynaldo stuffs a small bag into the closet and spins to face me.

"Oh, Francisco, it's you," he says, and he slumps down onto his bed in the corner of the room. "I went to your house when I heard, but it was empty."

"Yeah."

"You're at San Sebastián now." It isn't a question.

I nod.

"I'm sorry, man. I asked Mamá if you could stay with us for a while, but you know how it is—nobody wants to give the police a reason to connect them with a drug arrest."

"It's okay." I mean, it's not, but what else am I going to say? "Can you keep some boxes of our stuff here until I can come back for them?"

"Sure." Reynaldo jumps up and follows me outside. He carries the boxes inside while I prop the wheelbarrow against the side of the house.

Back in his room, Reynaldo shifts the boxes into a neat stack. "I have to go." I don't want to stick around. I don't want to talk. "I'll come back for that stuff as soon as I can."

"Don't worry about it. I'll see you at school?"

"I guess. Yeah."

I probably can't even afford return bus fare, so I walk the whole way back to the prison. I don't hurry. I'm not ready to be back there. Not yet.

So I walk slowly, and keep my eyes on the sky. The clouds are these shifty threads pulled apart by high winds that can't decide which way to go. I make at least a half dozen wrong turns. I'm barely looking where I'm going.

I pass a row of cholitas sitting in a line against the concrete wall, hiding from the sun in a slant of shade cast by the high roof of a government building. Their legs stretch straight out from their bright, tiered skirts. The soles of their feet are black from the grit of the city.

My feet just stop moving. I lean into the concrete and slide down beside the women. They all look at me, and the one closest to where I'm sitting reaches out and pats my hand. She says something in Quechua, and I don't even bother telling her I don't understand. I just sit there. My eyelids peel back and the world goes fuzzy at the edges.

After seventeen years of raising her son, my mother just takes off one day. I didn't want to believe it, but it's true. My mother is gone.

The carved wooden doors leading into the prison are wide open, and there's no line to get in, so I go straight up to the guard in the green jacket sitting behind a white plastic table. I didn't see this one yesterday.

"Name?" the guard asks.

"Francisco Quispe Vargas."

"Sign here."

I do, and he watches me the whole time. What—does he think I'm sneaking drugs in here or something? I'm not that stupid.

He waves me past, but I can feel his eyes on my back the whole way through the courtyard. I can't get used to having guards with guns around all the time, just looking for a reason to bust me. It's got me constantly looking over my shoulder, like I'm being hunted or something.

When I come back through the prison gate, Papá and Pilar are waiting for me. Pilar's got this look on her face that's angry and hurt and . . . I shake my head, and there it goes—any hope she was hanging on to, gone.

I sit beside my father and sister on the concrete and watch the prisoners milling around the courtyard.

I guess this is home now.

The prisoners are dirty. No matter what they were in their other lives or who they were before, they are all the same now. Papá was always meticulous about his looks. Combed hair. Trimmed and cleaned fingernails. Pressed pants. He always said, *Dress like the man you know yourself to be, not what the world thinks you are.*

Two days in here, and he is as filthy as the rest of them.

I guess I am too.

I go to the bathrooms to wash up before dinner. Bad idea. Raw sewage pours out of the faucet and all over my hands. I can't stop myself—I double over and throw up. My nose runs and my eyes sting from the bile, and dammit—we can't afford to waste food like that now. I wipe my hands off on a towel but the stink of somebody else's shit won't leave me.

Papá, Pilar, and I sit in a corner of the courtyard. The government gives prisoners a few bolivianos to buy food each day. They don't give Papá any extra money for Pilar and me, just a glass of milk and slice of bread for each of us in the morning. But at night? If we eat, my sister and I are taking the food right out of his mouth. Maybe that's why all the prison kids look hungry all the time.

We've been given a hot plate that plugs into the wall so we can heat potatoes or boil water for coffee in the morning. Or, at least, we could if we had a pot.

So instead, Papá buys a bowl of soup from the communal vat. Pilar draws on the ground with a stick. Her cheeks are streaked with tears that dried up hours ago. Papá's hand rests in the part between her long black braids. They're lumpy and crooked. Neither of us really knows what we're doing weaving together sections of her slippery hair.

I've been slit down the middle and gutted because my mother left, and I'm practically an adult. What about my sister? She's only eight.

Who's going to be her mother now?

October 10

Papá and I used to argue every Sunday.

Some families went to Mass. Some watched the fútbol games. We argued.

"Francisco, my son, you are not applying yourself."

Every Sunday, the same thing. My weekly homily.

"Your grandfather worked in the mines his entire life. When he came home at night, the pores of his face were filled with soot."

I would just roll my eyes. I'm good at that.

"His lungs, Francisco, were full of tiny bits of stone. He never, in the whole of my memory, drew in a full breath of air."

"Look, Papá, I'm sorry for him. But what does that have to do with me?"

A sigh. "I came to Cochabamba for the dream of you. I left the Altiplano and our ancestral way of life so that the children I would one day have could know better than a father dying a little bit every day."

"You've already done that—we're here. We're good. Why

do I need another year of school, Papá? I can read. I can write. Reynaldo and I have a plan—our shop is going to be great. You'll see."

And on, and on, and on. Every Sunday, the same thing. Except this one.

Today, Papá pulls me aside and says, "I paid a courier to take a letter to the post office; I wrote to your grandparents on the Altiplano. To their neighbors, actually, who can read and write. When they answer, I want you to take Pilar and go to live with them."

My head snaps up. No. No way am I living up there. "Papá, I don't know how to speak Aymara. I won't even be able to talk to them."

"You are a smart boy. You'll figure it out."

"There's no running water at their house. There's no electricity. There's nothing but rocks and llamas and a bunch of poor people."

Papá shakes his head. "Life in my parents' community is very different from our modern life in the city, that's true. But it's a good life, all the same."

"There's no secondary school up there. Just yesterday, and *every single day* of my life before that, you said I have to finish secondary school! You want me to stop now, when I have only six weeks left?"

Papá's sigh is like the last wheeze out of the organ pipes in the cathedral. "That was before your mother left. Francisco, you and your sister cannot live here." His eyes are wide and a little wild as they scan the courtyard. "My children in prison? Absolutely not." He drags a hand down his face. "Nothing else matters now."

am not going up there. You can't take a kid raised in the city with grocery stores and banks and hospitals and paved streets, and then, just when he's almost ready to make something of himself, yank him back to the dark ages.

I'll figure something out. Papá left the Altiplano to make a life here. No way am I giving that up.

My full name is Francisco Guari Quispe Vargas. Straight down the middle: half Spanish, half Aymara.

I look like my father, though. Dark skin, long nose, eyes so brown they could be black. If you picked me up and dropped me in the fourteenth century, traded my school uniform for a tunic and a pair of llama hide sandals, I would fit right in with my ancestors.

Pilar, on the other hand, looks like my mother. Pale, small-nosed, slender. One of the elite. She's the one Papá should spend his dreams on. Not me.

Mamá with her mestiza complexion and her middle class diction could have done so much better than a taxi driver. How did she ever let herself fall in love with a campesino like him—fresh from the Altiplano, still dropping Aymara phrases in with his Spanish? Did he write her love poems? Did he serenade below her window? Did he scatter the ground at her feet with petals?

All this time, was Mamá ashamed of the home she kept? Was she humbled by lovestruck poverty? Was she waiting, all this time, for a reason to leave?

October 11

P apá is already sitting and leaning against the wall when I wake up. I don't even get a minute to pretend that the prison doesn't exist, and that I'm still at home in my bed. My shoulders and hips ache where they pressed against the bare floor all night—and I guess the air would have given it away anyway. The stink of this place infects my dreams.

Papá watches me rub the sleep from my eyes. Last night's argument still hides in the creases and shadows of his face.

"Papá, come on, you can't be mad at me first thing in the morning."

He whispers his answer, so Pilar might sleep a little longer. "Francisco, it's not safe here. Think of your sister. She *cannot* live in a men's prison. Just yesterday, on my way to the toilets, I passed a cell with men crowded around the door. You know what was going on inside? Two boys were fighting each other. For entertainment. Like cocks in a pen, they were being paid to fight."

I sit up with a groan and scoot over next to Papá. I'm going to have bruises from the ground if we keep this up. "Look, I'll find work and rent a room in the city somewhere. Pilar can come live with me."

"And what job are you going to get that will pay rent for you both?"

"Reynaldo and I will just set up our shop sooner than we planned."

"Francisco, where are you going to get the money to start a business like that?"

"I don't know—I'll work in a bank like Mamá until Reynaldo and I can buy the cleats and stuff to get us going."

"Your mother had a university degree in accounting, Francisco. It took both of our paychecks to rent the home you grew up in. Even if you get a room in a cheap house, how are you going to pay next year's matriculation fee for Pilar? How are you going to afford her school supplies? Why do you think so many young married couples still live with their parents? It is very expensive to make it on your own out there, Francisco. And where would Pilar be while you are at work? Walking herself to school? Waiting for you in a house you share with strangers? Or is she working too?"

Okay, so I haven't really thought it through. "Fine. When Abuela and Abuelo answer your letter, she can go with them, and I'll stay here and figure something out for you and me."

"No. I won't have my family broken up any more than it has to be."

"I'm not living up there, Papá."

"Well, you can't stay here. I won't allow it."

"Great. So I guess I'll go live on the street. With the pick-pockets and glue sniffers. That's what you want?" I'm not whispering anymore.

"What I want is for my children to be safe. I want what's left of our family to be together. Why is that so hard for you to understand?"

Too late, we notice that Pilar isn't sleeping at all. She's watching us, her wide brown eyes darting between our faces, her doll clutched below her chin. I feel a slither of something moving through the empty space where things like lungs and a stomach and a heart used to sit under my skin.

Nobody's even asking her what she wants.

Entire families live in the prison. The mother usually goes out during the day to the cancha, where she sells handcrafts or the furniture made by the prisoners. The father usually works in the wood shop, or in one of the prison jobs: delivering messages from the outside or running one of the little stores in the courtyard. Some serve as delegates on the council that runs the place from the inside and reports to the guards on the outside. They take care of everything from discipline when a prisoner has earned it to collecting rent for the cells to keeping track of the kids who live here.

Papá asks me to watch Pilar while he goes to the back of the prison to talk to the guy who runs the wood shop. It's almost time for school, so I make sure Pilar's okay, then duck into the bathroom for a minute to change into my uniform.

But when I get back to the courtyard, I don't see Pilar anywhere. I turn in a slow circle, and the blood starts banging in my ears. All I hear is panic.

She was just here.

I break into a run. She's not in the courtyard. She's not in the bathroom. She's not in any of the rooms off any of the hallways.

She was just here.

I pound up the stairs and onto the second floor. I bang through every open door, and everyone inside is yelling at me. I'd be yelling too, if I could get any sound past my throat. I'm running and running, and there's this crowd watching me now, and I can't move fast enough.

Where is she?

The balcony is jammed with people, and I'm trying to push past them, but I can't—there are too many of them. I take a breath—I don't know, to scream? And in that half second of quiet, I hear this whimper, and it's not that I know that sound, not from her, but it registers somewhere in my spine. It scrapes over my skin.

I throw myself against the cell door where I think the sound came from. Hinges groan, wood creaks. Again. Again. I'm out of breath and my shoulder is pain and Papá is beside me now, and his face—

I throw myself at the door and this time the lock rips away from the door frame and I fall through and I can't stop myself from crashing to the ground. Pilar is in the corner, shaking, and there's a guy in the opposite corner, shielding his face from the splintering door.

Papá rushes in behind me and he has her.

He has her.

He's lifting Pilar into his arms and he's smoothing the shivers from her shoulders and he's wiping the tears from her cheeks and he's carrying her out of here.

"Did he hurt you?" Papá asks. "Did that man lay a hand on you?"

Pilar's face is tucked against Papá's neck and her eyes are squeezed shut and she shakes her head, no.

I pick myself up off the floor, and that guy is backed into the corner and saying something about a misunderstanding, but the blood is back in my ears and his words aren't even words. I swear, if I had anything more than my fists, he would be dead.

I don't get more than two steps toward him before I'm flanked by a half dozen prisoners. They push into the cell and move me out onto the balcony. I push back, I try to argue, but a mother on the balcony with two kids behind her skirts lays a hand against my chest, so calm, it stops me still.

"Let them handle him. A man like that is a danger to all of our families. Let them make their own justice in there."

I'm shaking. Every inch of me. The woman drops her hand, and I back away. The sound of fists on flesh follows me down the stairs as I hurry to catch up with Papá. They must have stuffed a sock in that guy's mouth, because I don't hear anything from him but these choked, drowning sounds.

I guess sometimes it's a good thing the guards stay outside the prison walls.

When Pilar was three years old, she idolized me. She'd follow me everywhere on her stubby legs, yammering nonstop. We couldn't understand half of what she said. She couldn't even say my full name yet, just Isco.

I'd take the trash out to the burn pile, and she'd trail after me. "Isco, Isco." I'd walk to the corner to buy some eggs, and she'd wait for me at the gate, her face pressed between the bars. As soon as I came into view, she'd start waving her arms and yelling my name. "Isco! Isco!" I'd take a bucket of soapy water outside to wash the windows of Papá's taxi, and she'd chase the bubbles that escaped into the air, laughing when they popped between her fingers.

One day I left the gate open when I went to play fútbol with Reynaldo. Pilar had been following me around the house all day, and I just wanted a minute to myself. When I came home, tired and sweaty, a couple hours later, Papá was holding Pilar, cradling her head and murmuring into her hair.

She'd followed me until she couldn't walk any farther and then curled up in the shade with a stray dog. My parents found her after an hour of searching, frantic, all over the neighborhood. When Mamá picked her up, Pilar had cried my name and pointed the way I'd gone.

Mamá didn't talk to me once that night. I tried to tell her it wasn't my fault. She didn't believe me, and I don't even know if I did either. After that day, I never left the gate open again, but still, I never thought twice about taking off without Pilar any chance I got.

Papá is holding Pilar now, just like he did that day, cradling her head and murmuring into her hair. There shouldn't be anything left inside of me to hurt, no organs to rupture, no tissue to tear. But it's like everything is busting open all over again.

Before the gate opens for the day, a body is dumped, barely breathing, in front of the guard station. The prisoners all watch as the guards come in and carry it away on a stretcher.

"He won't be coming back here, unless it's to the dungeon," says the prisoner standing behind Papá. "The guards will take him to the hospital, and unless he dies, they'll cover it up. The council will make sure of that."

Papá hands Pilar to me, and I tuck her against my side so she's looking away from the rows of prisoners. "Is she all right?" I whisper.

Papá closes his eyes and lets out a long, slow breath before he joins the rest of the men. "She will be."

When it's time for school, Papá puts Pilar's hand in mine and lays his over both of ours. I feel a shift in that moment: my limbs fusing to my sister's like they don't even belong to me anymore.

"Francisco, inside or outside of these walls, your sister is your responsibility. Other than the mornings at school, never let her out of your sight."

Pilar has stopped shaking, but her eyes are dull, and her steps slow. Before now, I would have felt like an idiot holding my sister's hand all the way to school. But this place is all dark corners like wells a person could fall into and never come out of again. Yeah, I'll take care of her.

I will.

Papá raises a hand in good-bye and watches us walk through the prison gate. I glance back before we turn the corner and he's out of sight. He looks like the loneliest person in the world.

The prison is on the opposite side of school from our old neighborhood, so I don't see anyone I know on the way there. We're like a pack of street dogs—all the prison kids walking together. Only we're not together. I don't even know most of their names. The kids who live in the women's prison across the plaza fall in with us, and I notice for the first time how few girls live in the men's prison. Only four, counting Pilar.

It takes us half an hour, the big, noisy pack of us. Half an hour of trying to figure out what to say to Pilar to make her feel safe in her own skin again. Half an hour of trying not to think about what's waiting for me at school. Half an hour of new streets and kids I don't know but who I guess are just like me.

When we reach the primary school, Pilar doesn't want to let go of my hand, so I kneel down in front of her and rest my hands on either side of her face, like Papá would do. I wait until she meets my eyes.

"I'll be right here when school gets out, okay? My school gets out thirty minutes before yours, so I'll be here when you're done. You wait for me right here."

She nods. Her eyes are round and wide, and if there were anywhere I could take her that would be safer than leaving her here at school, I wouldn't make her go in there alone, not today.

But there isn't. There's nowhere for us to go.

I wait to make sure she gets in okay and then head a few blocks over to the secondary school and through the double doors at the front. Guys lean on the half wall, flirting with the girls who sit there swinging bare legs under their skirts. I keep my eyes down as I pass through the crowd.

Does everybody know about Papá? Are they all talking about me behind my back?

There's only one way to find out. I walk up to Arturo and Mauricio and the rest of the guys. They don't say anything. They don't call me names or push me away. But they won't look me in the eye either.

"Hey, Reynaldo," they say when he walks up behind me.

But still, not a word to me. It's like I'm a leper or something, except they're not afraid their fingers or their noses are going to start falling off. They just don't want themselves—or their families—connected in any way to someone who was arrested on a drug charge.

"I get it, okay." I do. "But do you have to be such bastards about it?" They glance around at one another, but they won't look at me.

I drop my books to the floor and ram my way into their little circle. "Do you?"

"Francisco!" Reynaldo steps between me and them and throws an arm across my chest, pulling me away and slapping me on the back. He picks up my books and steers me away from them, from that fight.

"It's all right, man. We're almost out of here. You can ignore those idiots for a couple of months, right?"

I shake the fight out of my arms and take my books back. Walking away isn't something I do. But I don't want to hit my friends. Or even, I guess, my ex-friends. "Yeah."

He doesn't take his hand off my shoulder until they're out of sight. "Yeah."

got into my first fight when I was eight.

Two boys cornered me before school and called me *indio bruto*. I didn't know what it meant, but I saw the twist of their lips, their mocking eyes. So I rammed the bigger one in the stomach and knocked him to the ground, which gave the other one the chance to kick me over and over again from above.

It was Reynaldo who pulled them off, who looked away while I wiped the tears from my cheeks, who dusted the dirt from my uniform so the teacher wouldn't punish me for bringing dirt from the street into the classroom.

That night, Mamá and Papá sat me down on the sofa. I remember their knees touching mine, their arms encircling me, and the soft light from the lamps sinking into the carpet. I told them what happened, and Mamá was furious.

"I'm calling your teacher right this minute! Those boys don't know what they are talking about. They will be punished for what they said to you."

Mamá went into the kitchen and yanked the phone off the receiver. Through the open doorway I could see her fist on her hip, the round swell of her pregnant belly and the long loop of the phone cord swinging, agitated, around her knees.

Papá patted my hand and spoke in a soft voice. "My son, no person can make you feel inferior in this world unless you let them."

I remember looking up into his face, and not understanding what I saw there.

"Are you ashamed of the color of your skin? Are you

not proud that half of your blood comes from your mother's ancestors and the other half from mine? Is that not a beautiful thing? Do not both cultures have something honorable to impart?"

I don't know how I answered him that night. But the next day when the same boys taunted me again, I remembered my father's words. I told the boys that I was proud to be half Aymara. They just laughed and kicked dirt all over me, until it sank into the fibers of my woolen vest and coated my thick, black hair.

The teacher did punish me then, for being dirty a second day in a row. So I found the boys after school. I found my fists, and they never bothered me again.

The thing is, once you start fighting, it's almost impossible to stop. I'm not gentle like Papá. I'm not pale-skinned like Pilar. I'm not cultured like Mamá. I can play fútbol, and I can fight. It's not a bad thing to be realistic about what the world holds for you.

B esides my ex-friends, the rest of the day goes on as normal, when absolutely nothing is normal. Everything is upside down.

I have classes with pretty much the same kids I've gone to school with my whole life, except every year the group shrinks as a couple drop out. Most make it through primary school, but it's pretty rare for kids from our neighborhood to graduate from secondary.

So it's a small class now. There are my ex-friends, whose life is fútbol and who only stick it out here because their parents make them. There's a pack of guys who are super smart and always sit at the front of the class. Then there are the girls who are all bunched into one group because there are hardly any of them left. Except this one girl who always sits alone at the back, in every single class, and never says a word. I don't think I've ever seen her crack a smile.

And still there are tests and stupid scuffles between class in the sterile hallways lined with classrooms. And homework.

Are they serious? I am *really* supposed to do homework? In prison.

In algebra, Profesor Muñoz has his back to us, the chalk spitting dust into the air as the problem shifts and grows diagonally across the blackboard. He is talking while he writes, but I don't hear any of it—my mind just keeps rolling over the same unsolvable equation: Papá. Pilar. Me.

A row of barred windows lines the classroom wall, too high for me to see much out of. Bars at school, bars at the prison. Walls around me all the time. Little slivers of the sky.

This can't really be my life now.

School gets out at noon, and I go to the bank where Mamá worked, even though I know she's long gone. I stand at the picture window looking in; her station is empty. I knew it would be—so it shouldn't hurt to see it. But it does. It's like a knife sliding under my skin and slicing the cords and cables holding me together.

The glass door swings open. "Francisco, is that you?"

I shouldn't have come.

"I heard what happened to your father."

I push away from the glass and turn back toward the street. I can't quite look at her, this woman who's not my mother, dressed in the same tight blazer and clunky heels Mamá wore to work every day.

"I'm sorry to bother you," she calls after me, "but your mother hasn't shown up for work. I covered for her today. When can I tell the manager she'll be back?"

I turn my head, but I don't look back. "You haven't heard from her at all?"

"No. Why?"

I kick the dirt at my feet. "Mamá is gone."

She doesn't have an answer for that, so I just go.

"I'll talk to the manager and have her last paycheck sent to your father at San Sebastián as soon as I can, okay?"

I throw something like thanks over my shoulder and step into the street, dodging cars. Yeah, we'll take the money. It's not like we're above begging now.

collect Pilar from the primary school. She is still hiding inside of herself. I take her hand, gently.

We have five and a half hours until the prison gate closes and until Papá will be expecting us. I've lived in Cochabamba my whole life. I used to stay out all afternoon, roaming the streets with Reynaldo and hopping pickup games. Those were my streets; I knew them and they knew me. Nothing could touch me.

But it's different now, with Pilar to take care of and no home to go to if she gets tired or hungry or scared. Now I'm like a stranger in my own city—I don't know where to look, where to go, how to find my way.

We go to the big Catholic church on the corner and lie down on the pews. I'm asleep maybe even before my eyes close. But then the whole place starts shaking—no, I'm shaking. My eyes open in a squint. A priest is right in my face.

"Get up." He shakes me again. "You can't sleep here."

He moves to wake Pilar, and I stumble off the pew and jump in between him and my sister.

"Don't touch her." I grab Pilar's hand.

"Come on," I whisper.

I help her to stand, and we walk out into the bright afternoon, both of us blinking back the sunlight. Did I even shut my eyes for five minutes?

Pilar jams her fist into her eye socket and starts to cry.

"It's okay." What a stupid thing to say. Of course it's not

okay. I pull an old napkin out of my pocket and hand it to her. "Should we go to the park?"

The napkin takes the place of her fist, but she doesn't answer my question.

"Come on, Pilar, I'm trying. Tell me what I can do."

She's still not talking. Not a word since we found her in that cojudo's cell. I think maybe she's hungry, so I dig in my backpack for a few bolivianos and take her to a trancapecho food cart. She might stop crying if she eats something.

I pay the guy and she takes a bite, and sure enough, the tears stop. But there's this stretchy thing going on at the sides of my eyes, like my skin doesn't know how to fit over my bones anymore.

I can't hold myself together and somehow her, too.

make sure we're at the prison gate fifteen minutes before it closes for the night. The only thing worse than sleeping in that prison would be getting stuck out on the streets.

Papá is waiting for us just inside the gate. Pilar runs to him, and he takes her in his arms. He looks at me, his eyebrow raised in a question.

I nod in return. "We're okay." And then, because the mood could use a little lightening, "School was boring—what did you expect?"

Papá pulls us into a corner. We sit together while he unwraps three boiled potatoes and hands one to each of us.

"I had a big lunch," I say, in part because I'm not sure he's eaten yet today and in part because a cold potato for dinner sounds disgusting.

Papá gives me a look. "Eat."

So I do. It's food. I should be grateful.

My father grew up eating potatoes with every meal, every single day of his life. But even he's having trouble getting his dinner down tonight.

The council of prisoners that runs this place from the inside appoints one guy to oversee all the kids in San Sebastián. He finds us after dinner and hands Papá a dingy business card that lists the address and phone number of a day care center outside the prison.

"This is an organization that takes in the prison kids after school," he says. "It's a nonprofit, so you won't have to pay. The kids get lunch and help with homework and somewhere to spend their afternoons besides here."

Papá takes the card, his fingers smoothing out the creased corners.

"But just the girl can go."

"Why not my son? He's in school too. He needs a safe place to be."

The man wiggles his finger side to side. "The day care isn't set up yet to accommodate older kids. Maybe someday they'll get together a program for teenagers. Maybe not. I don't know."

Papá runs his hands through his thick black hair. "That doesn't help us. My son will turn eighteen in December."

The man lifts his palms to the sky. "It's not fair, I know. They appoint a new police officer to act as prison director every six months, to weed out corruption, they say. All that really means is the rules change in here all the time. Just when you get used to something, it changes. If I were you, I'd let the girl go while she still can."

Papá slips the card into his shirt pocket. "Thank you for your assistance."

When he's out of earshot, Pilar, who's been quiet—scary quiet since this morning, latches onto Papá's arm. "Please, Papá. I don't want to go. I want to stay with you."

"That's not possible, *wawitay*. I have to work, and you can't come to the wood shop with me."

Pilar drops her head like a bull in a ring. "Then I want to stay with Francisco."

Papá looks at her, and what moves over his face is like heavy clouds over the sun. "I don't know. I think maybe this day care will be better—"

I cut in. "I could take her there every day after school, and I could get a job in the afternoons. I could help pay the rent for a cell. Please, Papá."

"No, Francisco. Until we hear back from your grandparents, what you have to do in the afternoons is study."

It's like nothing has changed, even though everything has changed. My whole life has been flipped upside down, and here we are, arguing about me finishing school. We're living in actual hell, and nothing has changed.

"But Papá—"

"I won't do it." Pilar says. Her eyes dart between Papá and me. "I won't go."

Papá frowns. Is he thinking about how his older brother left home for the mines, and his older sister left to be a servant, and how he eventually left, too? How his parents were all alone, in the end?

"Perhaps you are right. We've had enough separation in

this family." Papá takes Pilar's face between his hands. "Very well, then. Your brother will take care of you in the afternoons. He will keep you safe."

I get this look from Papá. He doesn't want to say it, not in front of Pilar, why it is that suddenly her safety is everything. But he doesn't have to. I get it.

October 12

On the way to school in the morning, Pilar stops in the middle of the street. I tug at her hand and check over my shoulder to make sure a car isn't going to flatten us.

"What are you doing?"

She doesn't answer me, but her fingers trace the edge of a ribbon, blackened with sludge and patterned by the tread of passing tires. The rest of the kids pass us by.

"Pilar, that's dirty, don't touch—" Gross. Of course she has to pick it up. I tug again at her arm, and this time she comes with me, rubbing the discarded ribbon between her fingertips.

"Don't put that thing in your hair."

She twists her lips to the side. "I'm going to wash it in the sink at school. Aren't you curious what color it used to be? Or who it belonged to?" She holds the ribbon up to the sun and squints.

"Whatever it was, it's trash now."

Pilar stops again, still in the middle of the street. "This ribbon belonged to somebody once. She braided it into her hair, and it made her feel special. Don't you think that's still in there somewhere? Don't you think it's worth saving?" Her voice rises until it cracks.

I get her moving again, but all the way to the primary school, she just stares at that ribbon. I'm relieved she's talking, but I'm so mad at Mamá and that bastard at the prison and the whole world it's like a fire is eating me from the inside and all it's going to leave behind is hollowed-out bones for the wind to knock around.

M y writing teacher, Profesora Ortiz, begins a poetry unit. We read García Lorca and Neruda, Bedregal and Mistral. She talks about rhythm and sound, rhyme and all that a poem says under the surface.

With ten minutes left in class, she says, "All right, your turn. With the five weeks of school we have left, each of you will write and revise two poems per week. I won't be administering an end-of-year exam or assigning a lengthy essay. All you have to do is give yourselves over to these ten poems." She stops talking and sits on the edge of the desk, her arms crossed over her chest, the tip of her reading glasses clamped between her teeth, waiting.

I used to write poems all the time when I was a kid. As soon as I could read, Papá started leaving poems in my room for me, like a game of hide-and-seek. And as soon as I learned how to write, I started answering his poems with some of my own. As I got older, I figured out how to play a rhyme for a laugh, how to break up a line for a surprise. I knew exactly how to make my father smile.

It was our thing.

Somewhere along the way, I stopped. I don't remember why. Now it's been years since I've even tried. But Papá has never given up on me, no matter how long I've been silent in return. Until prison, that is. He hasn't written me a single poem since we got here.

I stare at the empty lines on the page in front of me while

all around, the sound of pencils scratching against paper grows as loud as hot rain on the roof.

Just write something stupid. Something about fútbol, or school, or food.

But nothing comes. That kid who knew how to think in poems is long gone.

The bell rings, and I can't get out of class fast enough. I sling my backpack over my shoulder and weave through the crowd, heading for the patio before every inch fills with students sitting on the tables and leaning against the brick wall that wraps around the small space.

Reynaldo bumps from group to group. His eyes find me and his head flicks up, but he doesn't come over, not yet. Instead, he turns his back to the door so his body hides what he's doing from the teachers chatting in the doorway. The transaction is quick—small packets exchanged in a subtle switch of clasped palms and hands slipping into deep pockets.

And then he walks away like nothing happened and comes to stand in the corner with me. I should be grateful. Reynaldo is the only one of my friends who acts like I still exist. So I should let it go.

But I don't. "What was that? What are you into?"

"Don't worry about it."

"Rey, come on."

"I found a way to get us a little money to start our shop,

okay? Forget the cancha, we'll get a storefront with a room upstairs where we can live. It'll be great."

"Don't get yourself in trouble for me."

"Look, we both know you won't be pitching in any money for our shop now. If it's all on me, how else am I supposed to get us going?"

"Rey—"

But he just starts talking about some girl he met at the movies last weekend. I lean against the bricks and nod my head every now and then, but I'm not listening. I'm barely here. What I thought my life was—what I thought it could be— none of it is real anymore.

My bones grind to dust, scattering on upward gusts of air.

When I pick up Pilar after school, her teacher is waiting to speak with me. And she doesn't look happy.

"Good afternoon, Profesora."

"It is a rule of this school that pupils must be clean."

Pilar won't look at me. Her hands are clasped behind her back, her fingernails digging into her palms.

"Yes, Profesora. I understand."

"I have been made aware of your family's situation. I am also aware that there are showers in the prison."

"Forgive me, Profesora, but there is no privacy for my sister in the showers. We live in a men's prison."

The teacher's lips pinch together. "If Pilar is not clean, she cannot come to school."

My sister doesn't deserve this. She's been through enough. "Please, Profesora, it isn't safe."

"I am sure you will find a way."

Pilar's eyes are bright, and her face is red with shame. I drape my arm over her shoulders. "We'll see you tomorrow, Profesora."

Pilar's head ticks up a notch, and we walk away together.

We go straight to the plaza a few blocks over, the one with the fountain at the center. We set down our backpacks, kick off our shoes, and get in fully clothed. We don't have any soap, but we scrub our hair and our clothes and our skin until we've gotten rid of half the grime. When we finally get out, we're sopping wet and we smell like old pipes, but it will have to do.

Pilar holds up a dripping fistful of bolivianos and foreign

coins the tourists tossed into the fountain. "We won't be eating cold potatoes for dinner tonight!"

The sunlight dances on the water slicking off her skin, and her teeth are bared in more of a grimace than a grin. The coins will buy us dinner; it's not enough to pay for a cell or a mattress, or even a couple of pillows. But it's something.

We lie on our backs on the stone rim of the fountain, head to head, Pilar's hair splayed out like the dropped leaves of a puya plant and curling at the ends. I don't know what to say to make it better. I never do. So I reach my arm back and ruffle her hair and hope she knows I've got her, no matter what.

Papá is waiting for us when we pass through the gate and emerge, blinking, into the bright sun of the prison courtyard. He squeezes my shoulder, and his other arm curls around Pilar.

"How was school today, *wawitay*?" He gets a shrug in return. "And what did you and your brother get up to after school, eh?" Another shrug.

Papá meets my eyes over Pilar's head. I wish my sister would go back to chattering about anything and everything all day long, because maybe that would mean something inside her isn't horribly broken.

When it's time for roll call, the prisoners line up in the courtyard, packed together in messy lines while the guard in the flat green hat runs down the list on his clipboard. Most days it's quick, but sometimes they have to stand there in the sun while the guards go through the list three times to get the count right.

I'm watching closely this time, sorting the prisoners into sets and learning their names. Most are like Papá, just caught in the wrong place at the wrong time and too poor to buy a day in court.

But there are others—real criminals. I try not to think about what they must have done to get put in here. Try not to think about the money Papá will have to spend just to buy protection for us from men like that.

Roll call happens every day, so it should be no big deal,

but every time the guards come inside and line up to face the men they're charged with keeping there, the tension in the whole place hikes up. The guards don't like being inside the prison any more than we like having them in here.

They don't trust us, and we don't trust them.

Before dark, Papá, Pilar, and I claim our little corner against the prison wall. We lie on our backs with our coats draped over us like blankets and our backpacks under our heads.

All evening, the same tired argument has buzzed back and forth between Papá and me like a fly you can't swat.

"Look," I whisper, "I get it. It's not safe here. But if we had a cell, it would be better."

Papá rubs his eyes. "Francisco—"

"Give me a week. If we aren't in a cell with a lock on the door by the weekend, I'll take Pilar to Abuela and Abuelo, whether they're ready for her or not."

My father sighs. But he doesn't answer, and he doesn't argue anymore.

October 13

On the way to school, Pilar's head hangs so low I can't see any part of her face.

I bump our clasped hands against her shoulder. "What?"

She shakes her head.

"What is it?"

Pilar chews on the side of her lip. "Do you think Mamá misses us?"

Shit. I should have known this was coming.

"Probably. Yeah."

"Then why doesn't she come back?"

"I don't know. Maybe she's afraid she can't, now that she's done this. Maybe she thinks we'll never forgive her."

"I could," Pilar says quietly.

"Yeah, well, I couldn't."

Pilar looks up at me finally, and her eyes are her whole face, round and brimming and so sad. "I miss her, Francisco."

I don't know what to do. I squeeze her hand, but she just

starts crying. Okay. Honesty, then. "I miss her too, Pilar. And I hate that more than I hate her."

Pilar grabs my arm with her other hand and rests the side of her face against my forearm. We walk that way, her leaning against me, all the way to school.

I've always been strong. I've always been fast. And even if I'm not tall like the rest of the guys, no one ever calls me little. But that's how I feel right now. Like a puny skin-and-bones weakling with all the blood and juice and all that was *me* seeping out onto the concrete.

Profesor Perez is talking about the War of the Pacific, how when our country lost its sea coast, we became isolated from the rest of the world. But that's ancient history, right? What's the point in getting all upset about something that happened a hundred years ago? It's the kind of thing me and my ex-friends would roll our eyes and laugh about between classes, if I were still talking to them, that is.

He segues into border disputes and the current state of diplomatic relations between Bolivia and Chile, and I stop even trying to listen. I don't need to know this stuff to open a fútbol shop. And nothing he has to say will fix the disaster that is my life now.

I kick the desk in front of me, and everyone turns around to stare. I shrink down in my seat and cover my eyes with a hand.

Mamá had a temper too. She always said I was too much like her for my own good. But what does it matter what she said? She gave up her chance to say anything to me. She didn't stick around long enough to get a say.

go outside between classes to get away from the crowd. I'm tired of pretending I don't notice my ex-friends ignoring me.

My back is to the door, and my face is tilted up to catch the sun where it floats, alone, in the middle of the sky. For a second, I could be anyone, anywhere. Just me and the wide-open sky.

Behind me, feet scuff against gravel, and before my mind registers what's happening, I get two quick jabs in the side. My eyes fly open, and my lungs seize. Whoever it is has a ring on.

I shouldn't have let my guard down. The guys go for my back and my ribs and my gut. They don't say why. They don't have to. I'm a prison kid now. I'm just trash to them.

My ribs are on fire, and my stomach has caved in on itself. But a fight has been coiling inside me tighter and tighter all week, just waiting for a reason to bust out—I'm almost glad they came at me now, when no teachers are around, and no one's here to stop us.

It's three on one, so anything goes. I aim for the nose and the jaw and the crotch and the knees, and I'm kicking and punching, and everything hurts. I'm slamming my fist into the meat of their faces and darting around like a bloodsucking mosquito so they can't pin my arms behind me. Watching the spit fly and their eyes go wide is like blood and bone and breath and life. They pummel me, and I beat the shit out of them, and for the first time since Papá was put in prison, I feel alive.

t's never worth it. The rush of the fight is gone the minute the adults pull you apart, and all you feel is empty.

For a few moments, I was alive. The prison, Papá, Pilar, Mamá—it was all gone. And then, as soon as the fight is over, everything goes flat, and the hurt on the inside is back. Only now, everything on the outside hurts too.

The worst thing, though, is knowing Papá will look at me with those eyes—so disappointed—like, how could this be my son? This violent, thinks-with-his-fists animal?

Why? he'll ask.

And I'll just shrug, because how can I tell him maybe this is all I'll ever be?

Papá doesn't want us hanging around in the prison while he's working and can't look after us. That's fine with me—I don't want to be in that place if I don't have to. But I still haven't figured out what to do with the hours after school and before the prison gate closes.

"Maybe I should take you to that day care place," I say to Pilar as we walk slowly along the sidewalk, me trying to hide my limp. "At least you could sleep—"

"No!"

I hold my hands up—*ow*. Beneath my shirt, my stomach is covered in blotchy purple and red bruises. I tuck my hands back into my pockets. "Okay, okay. I'll think of something."

Pilar takes my hand, but gently, so maybe I'm not hiding the fact that I got into a fight as well as I thought I was. We buy a couple of salteñas for lunch, and we eat slowly, to make them last and to trick our bellies into feeling full. We follow a pack of kids without uniforms—dropouts, street kids, walking like they know where they're going. They veer around a corner and under a low, crumbling arch, into an open courtyard. Dozens of kids sit on blankets in little shacks made of corrugated tin or around cookstoves on bare stone. It's like a little broken city filled with kids.

I don't know what this place is, but the hair rises at the back of my neck and I hustle Pilar away. We go to the cancha, even though staring at the stalls full of food we can't afford to buy makes my mouth water and an angry gnawing begin in my gut.

We walk past vendors displaying pyramids of ripe fruit or handmade llama wool sweaters or slaughtered animals hanging from the ceiling. Around the edges of the cancha, cholitas with tiered skirts, twin braids, and little hats sell food and handcrafts. Some of them carry babies in aguayo slings, while others heft cages of squawking hens or push wheelbarrows full of bananas.

There are always a few tourists hanging around the artisans' booths or taking pictures with cameras that cost more than my parents make—or, I guess, made—in a year. Their pale skin and tall frames stick out like flagpoles above the work-bent backs of the smaller, darker-skinned people all around them.

The cancha is every bit as crowded as the prison, and just as loud. But it doesn't have that cloud of hopelessness that hangs over San Sebastián. And as long as we keep moving, nobody bothers us.

That's about the best we can hope for now.

When we get back to the prison, Papá is waiting, and Pilar runs into his open arms. When I follow a few steps behind, still limping a little, Papá's head ticks to the side, and a long, disappointed sigh blows through his lips.

"It wasn't my fault, Papá."

His eyes fall closed, like it's too much to bear. Like this is going to be the thing that breaks him. Not prison, or his wife leaving. Me.

"They jumped me at school, while the teachers were inside. You have to believe me."

He nods, like he was expecting me to say something like that. While his eyes are still closed, other prisoners look me up and down as they pass. Some of them seem pained, like Papá, while others give me this look that's—I don't know—sizing me up.

I don't want respect from them, the prisoners who make a living running drugs. Or the ones with shifty eyes who know they've earned their place here, who know the outside world isn't anywhere they deserve to be. When I look at them, I understand why Papá would give up all he ever cared about just to get us out of this place.

October 14

F or our next poetry lesson, Profesora Ortiz talks about
cacophony and euphony and the soul of a word hiding in
the sounds it makes leaving your lips. And, yeah, I roll
my eyes with everybody else, but maybe living in the prison is
messing with me—cracking open something I sealed shut a
long time ago, because when the room falls into a silence thick
with unwritten words, this time I find a few of my own.

> *Papá is the poet in the family*
> *not me, not anymore.*
> *It's like he's dreaming*
> *the whole time he's awake.*

> *When I was young,*
> *we traded poems like kisses*
> *on the cheek.*

It's maybe half a poem. Is half a poem enough? I flick my
pencil between my thumb and forefinger like the blades on

a helicopter. Papá used to say poetry was like breathing, that each moment has its own cadence, and its own weight. Some moments are for little gasping breaths, and others for deep, gulping ones. He said the mountains breathe and the sky breathes and the ground beneath us breathes.

Okay. I look around the room, and everyone is writing, even the always-scowling girl at the back who doesn't usually bother with schoolwork.

Poetry is like breathing. Right.

> *I don't think like that anymore.*
> *But some days I almost pick up a pen*
> *to tell Papá the things I can't say out loud.*

Breathe.

> *The night before the night*
> *he didn't come home*
> *I had all these things*
> *I wanted to tell him—*
> *but I didn't.*

> *It's harder now.*
> *I don't know how to be that soft anymore.*

> *I don't think*
> *I have any of those kinds of words left.*

On a hill overlooking the city, there's this massive white statue—the tallest Cristo in the world. Usually, the only people on the wide stone steps leading up are tourists and penitents, but today Pilar and I go too, just to have something to do after school. To keep the prison at a little bit of a distance.

We don't talk on the way up. The rasping feeling in my lungs, and the burning in my quads is better than the empty ache under my ribs. It shuts up my mind, so at least for the climb, I can almost forget how sad Pilar is all the time now. I can almost forget about Mamá leaving and Papá stuck in San Sebastián, how there doesn't seem to be anything I can do about any of it.

Halfway up, Pilar misses a step and bangs her shin.

"Here, let me carry that for you." I lift her backpack onto my shoulders. Pilar rubs the spots where the straps dug in, where her white uniform is damp with sweat.

It doesn't come easy to me—thinking about her and what she needs. It's not something I ever did before. I never had to. She was just my little sister, always in the way, always in my space. She had my parents to take care of her. It wasn't all up to me.

"You okay?"

She nods.

"We're going to get through this, Pilar. I don't know how, but we will."

She doesn't look up; she just keeps climbing the rocky steps. She probably doesn't believe me. I don't know why she would.

The higher we climb, the more the air below us grows

hazy, and the sky sort of glows. When we get to the top, we don't bother with the statue that towers over us. Instead, we sit on a low stone wall and share his view of the city. Everything below seems tiny—just a mess of orange roofs and crisscross roads.

You can't tell the prison from the other thousands of buildings. Everything and everyone looks the same. Free or not, poor or not, from up here, everybody looks the same.

After a few hours, we head back down to the city. We take our time so Pilar doesn't fall again, and because it all seems a little better from a distance. I squeeze Pilar's hand and get a half smile in return.

"I'm going to get Papá's taxi back," I say. "I'm going to figure this out."

And if the look I get isn't full of confidence, I guess I deserve that. I haven't been the best brother in the world. I haven't been dependable or even really all that nice to her over the years. But it's going to be different now. Everything is going to be different.

When we get back to the prison, I stop at the guard station between the wooden door to the outside and the gate leading in. They know my face by now—they let me come and go as I want, when the gate's unlocked, that is. So as we approach, the guard opens the gate with a warning.

"You better be quick. We're locking up in five minutes."

"Yes, sir. I just have one question."

The guard raises an eyebrow and waits.

"My father's taxi was confiscated when he was arrested, and I need to get it back. Can you help me find it?"

"Why are you asking me?"

"Because you're a policeman."

"Yeah, but I'm assigned *here*. I'm a police guard—I'm not involved in auto arrests. You need the Tránsito. They're the ones who patrol the highways."

"Okay. Thanks. I'll ask there tomorrow." I pull Pilar through the gate with me.

"It's not going to do any good. Property seized under the 1008 is never given back. That taxi's gone."

"What do you mean?"

The guard stares at me through the bars. "Ignorant, stupid indios," he says to the air as much as to me.

I take a step toward him, but then I stop myself. I shake out my hands.

"You need to back up," the guard says. "We're locking up for the night."

Before he shuts the gate, a figure pushes past us. I don't get a good look at his face, but there's something about the way he walks or the hunch of his shoulders that seems familiar. He quickly crosses the courtyard and disappears into a dark hallway, and a few seconds later, reappears on the balcony, unlocks a cell door and steps through.

Pilar runs to where Papá waits, and I relax a little, knowing there are two of us to look after her for the rest of the night.

Instead of sitting in a corner of the courtyard to wait for roll call like we usually do, Papá leads us up the back stair and onto the balcony. With his arm around Pilar, he takes the steps slowly. He asks her about school and where we spent our afternoon, and did we get something to eat? Pilar answers in shrugs and one-word replies, her head pressed against Papá's side.

Papá stops in front of a narrow door. "The money came

earlier today for your mother's last paycheck," he says. "It was enough to rent this cell for a few months."

He unlocks the door and steps back. Pilar walks through the door frame—it's only big enough for one of us to go in at a time. Papá stops me from following her with a hand on my arm. His voice is low, and pleading. "Just because we have a cell, that doesn't mean I want you to stay here longer than absolutely necessary. It doesn't mean prison is a good place for you to live."

"Papá, we're safer than we were yesterday. That's enough for now, no?"

"And what about your sister?"

I step into the cramped space. The cell is so small that a single dingy mattress for the three of us to share takes up the whole width of the room. The walls are chipped, and there's a space in the corner where someday we might be able to fit a stool, or a bookshelf or something. If we can afford it. There's a window near the ceiling, with bars, of course. But we can see a little rectangle of sky.

What really matters, though, is there's a door with a lock on it. Inside the cell, I feel my spine straightening. We shut the door and lock it, and we know Pilar will be safe in here.

Tonight we'll all be safe.

October 15

I n the morning, I drop Pilar at school and walk all the way across town to Reynaldo's to pick up the boxes. I should be at school too, but we can't wait until the weekend for the towels and the soap and the change of clothes in the boxes Mamá packed. Not when Pilar's teacher is all over her. Not when I know how bad Papá needs just a little something good right now.

Reynaldo's mother lets me in, and she doesn't try to talk this time. The wheelbarrow is still outside, and the stack of boxes is just where I left it.

I carry the boxes down the hall and out the door as quickly as I can, but not so fast I don't see the kitchen with a stocked refrigerator or the bowl of eggs and a dish of softened butter on the counter. The bathroom with a door for privacy. The living room with family pictures beside the sofa. All the reminders of what a home is supposed to be like.

I let myself out.

I'm already dirty—I haven't showered in a few days—and I'll be completely disgusting by the end of this. It's one thing to walk from the prison to our old neighborhood, and it's another to push a heavy wheelbarrow all the way back. The bigger roads have sidewalks but the side roads don't, and the wheel bumps all over the cobblestones and jolts into ruts. The dust and grit from the city cakes in the creases of my eyelids and elbows and knees.

The hills that have always been there, all around, seem scornful now, and the walls around every building seem a little higher, like it's me they're keeping out. Since when don't I belong in the neighborhood I grew up in?

I'm dripping with sweat and curses by the time I make it back to the prison. I carry the boxes up the stairs and stack them in the empty corner of our cell. There's no room for the wheelbarrow, so I take it to the cancha where I haggle with a thick-waisted cholita for a few extra bolivianos. I pocket the money and head to Pilar's school.

When she comes outside, I stuff her backpack inside mine and we head back to the prison. Papá doesn't want us there alone while he's at work, but we'll make an exception today.

We go straight to our cell and lock ourselves inside. Together we spread a sheet over the stained mattress and plant three pillows at the head.

When Papá finishes at the wood shop, it's like a holiday in here—the two of them *oooh*ing and *ahhh*ing over every little thing they pull out of the boxes, like an extra pair of socks or an old blanket is some amazing gift.

The whole thing turns my stomach, but I can't spoil it for them. So I grab a towel and a bar of soap and head to the back of the prison to shower. I'll feel better once I'm clean.

The bathroom is disgusting. There are two toilets in the prison for how many hundreds of us? And four showers. No way is Pilar showering in here. Ever.

Lukewarm water trickles down from a rusting showerhead, and I scrub and scrub, and the soap stings, so I know I'm getting clean, but this place is so vile I can't tell until I'm out in the open air and taking the stairs up to our cell two at a time. Then I can draw in a full breath. Then I almost feel like myself.

I give my wet head a swipe and toss the towel on the mattress where Papá and Pilar are still sorting through their things. I step out onto the balcony. The sun beats down on the courtyard, so the place is empty except for a circle of guys my age—the only ones my age who live in the prison—playing futbolito in the dirt, juggling a ball so flat it isn't so much bouncing from knee to foot to knee again as rolling from one limb to another. Pathetic.

It's something, though. A small piece of the life I had before the prison, and the one thing I really had going for me. I head downstairs, and the guys make a space for me in their circle, like I'm one of them, just like that.

The ball moves, and we move with it. Flick and tap and roll—the ball has a sloppy rhythm that our bodies mimic to catch and cradle and pass it on again.

When it hits the ground at last with a puff of dirt, the game pauses and everybody looks at me—the new guy—like they're waiting for me to say something.

I don't.

I think we're about to get the game moving again, but one of the prisoners walks across a corner of the courtyard and the guys all stiffen. His face is gaunt, and gray patches hide under the hard lines of his cheekbones. His shadowed eyes never seem to settle on anything.

The guys don't look at him, not directly, but I do. I've seen him before. He's the wiry one that walks with a hitch in his step—the one who pulled a knife on that prisoner outside the bathroom on my first day in here.

When he's out of sight, the kid from school—José—leans toward me and whispers, "Watch out for that man. They call him Red Tito."

"Yeah," says another guy with a raised scar on his collarbone. "He did something bad last year, and he landed in the dungeon for a month. None of the adults will say what he did. They just make sure we know to stay away from him."

The rest of the guys are nodding. And then they're all looking at me again, like I'm supposed to start talking.

But I have nothing to say.

"So what—they got your father on the 1008?" José asks.

Like he knows anything about my family. "Papá didn't do anything. He shouldn't even be here."

"Like he said," snaps the guy with the scar, "the 1008."

"Stop saying that." My head is pounding. I slap the ball off José's shoulder.

"What's your problem? It's the truth."

The words are barely out of José's mouth before my fist flies out and glances off his teeth.

In that second, I'm not just a sack of bones rattling around anymore. I can feel the muscles in my arms and legs and the blood coursing through them. I feel good. Really good.

It scares the shit out of me.

The circle closes around me, but José just wipes the grit off his lip, licks and spits the blood pooling on his tongue. He lifts his hands like a caught thief and slowly drops one onto my shoulder.

He says, "The 1008 doesn't care about innocent or guilty. It doesn't care about any of us. We're all in here because of that stupid law. Get used to it. Unless you plan to fight the whole world?"

I back away. Whatever blood and bluster my swinging fists called up is gone.

When I get back to our cell, Papá's eyes flick to my scraped and bruised knuckles. He jumps up and grabs me by the arms.

"What happened?"

Pilar looks back and forth between us.

"Nothing. It was just a little disagreement."

"Francisco, look at me." Papá waits until I raise my eyes to his. "This is not our old neighborhood, where scrapes and

scuffles are no big deal. You *cannot* fight here. Do you understand me? You cannot fight inside the prison. Do you want a
target on your back? Do you want to live in a place like this
your whole life?"

I shrug off his hands, drop onto the mattress, and turn
to the wall. If I was a skeleton before, I'm not even that now.
I'm nothing.

October 16

Waking up in prison is a shock, every time. But waking in a cell with only Pilar and Papá is better. It's almost privacy. It's almost safe.

They're both up already, heating water on the hot plate for some coca tea. Pilar is holding a half dozen cactus spines she collected yesterday in the plaza. I roll over, wince as I bang my bruised knuckles against the floor, and sit up. I drag over the box Mamá filled for me and begin unpacking. When I lift out my algebra textbook, a folded square of white paper tumbles to the ground.

I unfold the poem. I remember this one. Papá gave it to me a few years ago after I got into a fight at school.

I sneak a look over my shoulder, but Papá and Pilar aren't paying any attention to me. I guess that's our new version of privacy. No walls or doors or even a hanging bedsheet to divide the space. Just averted eyes, hushed voices, and bodies angling away from one another.

Out of Place

There are places in this world
Where a car with windshield wipers makes sense:
Cobija, for one.
London,
Laos,
Rio.

But here, all the wipers do
Is move the dust back and forth,
Smear sunlight across the glass,
Wipe the guts of all manner of bugs
Before my eyes.

How does a thing come to be so out of place
Where it has landed?
A polar bear in a Mexico zoo?
An air conditioner in Siberia?
My children in a city
Half mad with poverty,
Half mad with crime?

Does the polar bear shed his thick coat?
Does the air conditioner learn to give off heat?

Does my son forget
How kind his heart began in this world?

Yeah, Papá. I learned to fight. What else was I supposed to do?

All day, Pilar sits by herself, inside herself. Perched on a corner of the mattress, she draws overlapping circles on the ground with a rock. It doesn't make a mark on the concrete, but she doesn't seem to care. She just keeps drawing.

I never thought I would miss her constant questions. I guess I never imagined she could be like this.

"What are you making, Pilar?"

The circles don't stop, and she doesn't answer.

"Do you want me to find you a pen or something? You can have a page out of my notebook."

She still doesn't answer, so I scoot beside her and pick up a pebble of my own. Instead of circles, I draw overlapping clouds. Layers and layers of clouds crowding out the sky.

After roll call that night, Papá brings a glass of liquor he bought from another prisoner and performs a blessing in our cell.

I only remember him doing something like this twice before. Once when Pilar was born, and once when he bought his taxi. Maybe Mamá didn't want those kind of rituals in the house. Maybe he gave up that sort of thing willingly.

I don't know exactly what he's doing. But the words he's speaking are Aymara, and the alcohol he flicks into the air is so bitter it singes the inside of my nostrils. When he's done, he wraps his arms around our shoulders and pulls Pilar and me close.

"This is our home now."

I'm relieved that we have a cell with a door and a lock—I

am. But I can't bring myself to call this place home, and I can't fake happy. I carry our bucket downstairs and fill it in the sink at the back of the prison. I take my time, so I won't ruin Papá's moment.

When I get back to the cell, Papá and I lift up the mattress and lean it against the wall so there's an open patch of concrete floor. In the corner of our cell, we hold up a blanket so Pilar can bathe and wash her hair. When she's done, Papá combs through the tangles, the wet strands sticking to his wrist and twining around his fingers. As gentle as he tries to be, it hurts her—Pilar makes these little gasps every time the comb hits a knot.

She doesn't complain, though, and somehow that makes it even worse. I'm so mad at Mamá I can hardly see the teeth of the comb sliding between strands of Pilar's slick black hair. What kind of mother leaves an eight-year-old girl in a men's prison?

October 17

Today is Sunday, so the kids in the prison spend the morning playing, or doing homework, or going out with their trays of toys to sell. I sit with Pilar on the balcony in front of our cell and watch the prisoners and their families below.

Halfway through the morning, José comes in through the gate carrying grocery bags. I watch him move through the courtyard and reappear on the third level, letting himself into a cell in the far corner. The scrapes on my knuckles have scabbed over, but the skin around the edges will probably be red and swollen for days.

Pilar chews on the side of her lip while she watches the mothers cooking in the open courtyard, children running around their skirts and grabbing bits of food when the women look in the other direction. My sister has this hungry look on her face, but it's not the food she wants.

I can't do this anymore. I have to get out, even if it's just for an hour, to breathe in the unbroken expanse of the sky.

go to Reynaldo's, and he catches me up on what's going on in the neighborhood. I tell him how I'm going to get Papá's taxi back and how Papá wants me to take Pilar to live with my grandparents.

I don't tell him everything, though. Not how my grandparents are basically strangers to me. How after Pilar was born, Mamá rarely went with us to visit them again. How once Mamá stopped going, Pilar and I stopped too, until only Papá made the yearly trip to the Altiplano.

Reynaldo hasn't said it, and I haven't said it, but even though he hasn't dropped me like the rest, we're not the same as we were before. I'm a prison kid now. And he's—I don't know. He's different now, too.

Reynaldo hands me a catalog with all the new uniforms for next year's club championship in Brazil. The trick is to buy jerseys for the teams that have the best chance of going all the way, so you don't get stuck with a bunch of shirts for a losing team.

"It's going to be Manchester United and Real Madrid in the finals, for sure," Reynaldo says.

"What—you're just going to give up on the whole continent right from the start?"

He dips into his father's liquor stash, and for the rest of the afternoon, we take turns drinking straight from a bottle of cheap singani as we go back and forth, arguing about nothing, just so we don't have to talk about what's really going on.

know what I have to do when I get back. I'm not looking forward to it, so I take my time walking to the prison.

José shares a cell on the third level with his three little brothers and his parents. Before the sun goes down, I stand outside the door, where they can't see me, but I can hear them inside. It sounds like close spaces and overflowing smiles, like they've found a way to be happy because they're together, even though they live here.

I know that couldn't have been us—Mamá never would have settled for a life in prison. But it still stings to see a family that didn't break apart when the father landed here.

I step into the open doorway and knock on the frame. José jumps up when he sees it's me. The side of his mouth is bruised, and a deep red line slices down his lip.

I did that. Why did I have to do that?

I can't hear the exchange between José and his mother, but the way she looks at me—I can tell she knows. José steps outside and closes the door behind him.

I say what I came to say fast before I change my mind. "I'm sorry I hit you."

He leans back against the door frame and crosses his arms over his chest.

"You didn't deserve that. I don't know why I always . . . There's no reason for it."

José drops his arms and looks away from me. "Your mom ditched you in here, didn't she?"

Like I didn't already feel like shit, coming to him like this. But I guess I owe him some answers.

I nod.

"I'd be pissed too."

"Yeah. Still, I'm sorry. I shouldn't have taken it out on you."

"Okay."

I shove my hands in my pockets. "Okay."

And he goes back inside. Nothing has changed, not really. We're still stuck here, and Mamá is still gone. But maybe it'll be easier if I don't have to live with my own shit too. Not when everything around me is rotten, inside and out.

October 18

watch the gate when the police guard unlocks it Monday morning. A door opens down the balcony from ours, and the same figure in that floppy hat and baggy clothes hurries down the stairs, across the courtyard, and out of the prison. This time I get a good look at his face. Only it isn't a him I'm looking at—it's a *her.*

And I know who it is. I didn't recognize her at first as the always-scowling one in the back row of all my classes.

She's different from the other girls at school. She doesn't wear a tie knotted between her breasts or a vest buttoned tight over her ribs. No black underlining her eyes. Just her uniform (that always looks like she slept in it) and long socks up to her knees, a flat, unsmiling line for a mouth, and darting, aggressive eyes. And, yeah, if she has lived in here all these years, I get it.

She's the only teenage girl in the prison. Maybe the others had family they could go stay with. Or maybe they decided life on the street was better than this place. So why is she still here?

As I begin to turn away, a movement below catches my eye. Red Tito is lurking by one of the little stores, half in shadow and half lit by the morning sun, watching the gate and the figure who just passed through it.

After Papá sees us off, I pull a folded piece of paper out of my pocket. Since trying to talk to Pilar isn't going so well, I think maybe Papá's words will help.

I slow my steps so there's some space between us and the rest of the prison kids on the sidewalk—I don't want anyone else to hear this.

I unfold the paper, and Pilar peeks over my arm.

"Did Papá write that for you?"

"Yeah. A long time ago. Mamá packed it with the rest of my stuff." And I start reading. My voice cracks, and at one point it takes a whole block for my throat to open up again. But I read the whole thing out loud, and for a while at least, it's almost like Papá is there with us, outside the prison walls.

The Colt

Today's fare took me far outside the city
To the grounds of an old hacienda.

The buildings sagged with neglect,
Vines that had once been trimmed and trellised
Leapt from crevice to crack
Bearing a flower or cluster of grapes
Wherever they pleased.

The only living thing
Still trumpeting the exalted life of the hacendados
Was a colt, black as a mine shaft,
Sleek as a blanket
To swaddle a newborn child,
Proud as the men who brought his forebears
Across the ocean, in the belly of a ship
Laden with Spanish gold.

The colt ran beside me
As my dusty taxi crunched over the road
His tail aloft, his mane flicking defiantly
His hooves shucking tufts of sod behind him.

I wonder who brushes his coat to gleaming.
Who sits astride that tall back?
What son of a slave
Takes such pleasure in caring for the symbol
of a fallen master's reign?

When I finish reading and I tuck the poem back in my pocket, Pilar ducks her head under my elbow and wraps her arm around my hip.

We're going to be late if we walk more than a few steps connected like this, but I don't pull away. And, yeah, it's slow going, but it's worth it.

drop Pilar at school, but instead of going to class myself, I start the long walk across town to the Oficina de Tránsito. I shouldn't keep cutting school, but I don't want Pilar with me if this doesn't go well.

In Cochabamba, there are walls around every building, pushing people through the streets with these little breaks in the press and run of the city, grassy plazas with fountains and benches or little parks with stone statues every so often. When you walk through the neighborhoods, you can't see what's behind those walls—maybe just a peek at a second floor if there is one, or at the water tank on the roof. But the wall says enough about who lives behind it.

Is it just bricks mortared in place, or is it reinforced with custom metalwork? Is it crumbling stucco with graffiti showing through the paint, or has the outer layer been shaped into a decorative relief?

I'm walking, trailing my fingers over brick and then stone and then steel and then brick again. Memory blurs the sidewalk in front of me, and I'm right there, five years ago with Reynaldo, running back from a pickup game farther from home than we were supposed to go. I'd never seen such fancy stamped concrete sidewalks and walls lined with flowering trees that smelled like the perfume Mamá wore on special occasions.

At first we just knocked the ball back and forth a little bit while we ran, and the walls were like a third player. We jogged sideways, bobbing and winding each behind the other to keep the ball from hitting the ground.

And then we started to shoot, tentatively at first. The edges of the brick became our goalposts, but there was no chasing the ball if we launched it into the air and over the walls, so we took our running starts and carefully aimed for the corners. Laces down, knee over the ball, plant and strike.

I couldn't have been more than ten years old. I shouldn't have known then the difference between rich and poor. And I definitely shouldn't have felt the bitterness in the gap between the two. But if I didn't, why did it feel so good when I landed a solid hit?

I lift my fingers away from the wall and tuck my hands into my pockets. The neighborhood gives way to a row of businesses, and instead of walls facing the sidewalk, it's one roll-down metal door after another.

The police station is a four-story mint-green building. I walk up the steps, push through the door, and make my way to the front desk. The overhead light glances off my skin, and my shoes squeak against the linoleum floor. Two officers at the back of the room lean over an open file. I can hear the low murmur of their conversation, but I can't make out the words. One of them looks up and motions for the other to deal with me.

"Yes?" The officer's brows snap together as he approaches the front desk.

"I am here to see about my father's taxi. It was confiscated, and I need to get it back."

The officer hangs his thumbs from his belt loops. "Your father should be the one asking, not you."

"He can't." I swallow. There's no shame in just saying it. "They put him in San Sebastián. He would come if he could."

"We can't help you, then." The officer taps the desk once and walks away from me.

"Papá didn't do anything wrong. He's not a criminal." The other officer looks up. I'm shouting now. "If my father can't work, then I have to work in his place. How am I supposed to do that without the taxi?"

The second officer approaches. His hands are up in the air like he's trying to pacify a drunk or a crazy person or something.

"What my partner means is we *can't* help you. Tránsito probably made the arrest, but after that, these cases leave our department. If your father was arrested on the 1008, I'm sorry to say it, but the taxi is gone. You don't need the police; what you need is a lawyer."

I shake my hands out and blink back the heat.

Mamá said the same thing. I hate her for being right. And all over again, I hate her for leaving.

I don't even bother showing up late to school. I wait a few hours for Pilar, and we go to the plaza, where we lie down on one of the wooden beds in the street in front of the prison. Pilar stares at the clouds, clutching her doll against her stomach. I don't know if anything will bring back who she was before.

I can't help her, and I can't help Papá either. I've never felt so useless in my whole life.

After we go inside the prison, I watch for the girl from school. Sure enough, she's the last one through the gate before they lock it. She goes straight to her cell on the second level and doesn't come out again.

When Papá comes into the cell after roll call, he's holding my grandparents' letter. It says:

> Send the children to us—your father is too
> ill to travel. We will happily make a home for
> Francisco and Pilar here.

Papá sews a rectangle of fabric into the lining of my jacket and stitches money for bus fare to the Altiplano inside. He draws a map of the route out of the city, up to the high plains, and into my grandparents' community tucked into a fold of the mountains.

"Go tomorrow morning," he says. "Take your sister and go."

"Papá, no. We have a cell now. We're safer than we were before." I hate that I have to fight him on this.

"Francisco, you have to go. If not for me, then for your sister. Please."

Pilar's eyes dart between us. Her silence is deafening.

"There's nothing for me there. I'll take Pilar if you think it's safer for her, and if that's what she wants, but I'm not staying."

"Prison is not a good place for you, either, Francisco."

No. He can't make me. This place has already taken my mother from me, and my friends. My life—what's left of it—is here, in the city. If I give it all up to go dig potatoes and tend sheep on the Altiplano, it's over. My whole life is over. Doesn't he know how much I have to lose if I give up on everything here?

"Listen to me, my son. You have to leave."

"I don't want to go live with a bunch of *indios*, okay?"

My father takes a breath, the kind that moves in slow and sits heavy in the lungs. He drops his head and blows it all back out in a rush. "Sit down."

"Papá, I don't—"

"*Francisco!* Sit down."

My legs buckle, and I sink onto the mattress until my knees are level with my eyes. I wrap my arms around my shins, to have something to do with myself besides clenching and unclenching my hands.

"You're angry, Francisco. I see that. I ache for you and this anger that nips at you like a dog at your heels. You think my parents' way of life is an ignorant one, a worthless one in this modern world. But ignorance has many faces in this world. You will understand that someday. The most educated, polished, privileged person can be rotten with ignorance. And someone who never spent a single day inside a classroom can be full of knowledge you won't find in any textbook.

"You think I am who I am because I left that place and that way of life. But the truth is, I am who I am because I came from that place. You think I am kind? I learned that from my *indio* father. You think I am strong? I learned that from my *india* mother. You think I'm a poet because I left the Altiplano, because I chose not to lead the traditional life my parents and grandparents and great-grandparents led? My son, I am a poet because I *came* from the Altiplano, and the beauty and history and tragedy of that place is stamped on my soul."

October 19

I'm still not leaving, no matter what Papá says.

When he walks us to the gate in the morning, he places Pilar's hand in mine, kisses her on the head, and tells her, "Do not let go of your brother's hand. No matter how many miles separate us, you will always be my beloved daughter."

Then he rests his hands on either side of my face and looks up into my eyes. "My son, I hope with all of my heart that you do not return here tonight. Know that my dream of you will never fade. My love for you will never fail."

He's saying good-bye, like it's the last time he'll ever see us.

It's just—if I take Pilar to the Altiplano and come back to the city, where I can visit Papá in the evenings and find a way to get a lawyer, I've still abandoned her up there, and what— her education is over? Her chance at a modern life in the city is over? And if I stay with her, then I abandon Papá and any hope of a life for myself.

We all lose.

Pilar has a vine or something wound between the fingers of her right hand—I didn't even notice her pick it up this time on the walk to school.

"Papá's right, you know," I say.

Pilar looks up at me, questioning.

"It's not safe for you in the prison."

She nods, and her head drops again, her chin almost resting against her chest.

"I'll take you to Abuela and Abuelo now if that's what you want."

She doesn't answer.

"Should I try to track down Mamá? Maybe you could stay with her."

Pilar bites her lip. "No."

I drape my arm around her shoulder, and she leans against me.

"I want to stay with you and Papá as long as I can."

"Okay," I say. "Okay."

I look for the girl from prison when I get to school. She's already in her seat when I walk into algebra class; her hair is wet and dripping down the back of her white shirt. The backpack beside her chair bulges with the rolled-up lump of her shed overlayer.

She glances up, and I quickly look away, though the feeling of her eyes on me lingers. I want to look back again, and maybe say something. But I don't.

I stare at my desk. The bell rings. Profesor Muñoz starts talking, but I'm not listening.

Does she have any friends? How is it that I don't even know her name? Is she alone out there on the streets? Is her only defense in this world a set of baggy clothes to hide the shape of her?

After the last bell, I follow the girl as she leaves school. I trail half a block behind, on the other side of the street, weaving through the gaps between parked cars and street-side walls. It's not like I'm going that far out of the way to Pilar's school.

It's just—somehow this girl has figured out how to survive in the prison, and on the streets, apparently all alone. Okay, so I'm curious. What's wrong with that?

Two guys, older than me and not wearing school uniforms, step out in front of her. They're standing in a gap between parked cars, and I can see every feint and sneer, hear the bite and juice of their words, but I can't make out what they're saying. One of them slides beside her and reaches a hand under her skirt.

In that second, her whole being bristles. She yowls like a wildcat treed by a pack of dogs. Instead of slinking away and running down the street, she leaps at them and claws at their faces, aiming for the soft flesh of their eyes.

Run! I'm screaming inside. Why isn't she running?

But I don't say anything. I don't do anything. I just stand there. Bone fused to bone, locked in place by tendons that have forgotten how to bend and sway.

I never back down from a fight. But now, when someone could actually use my fists, I just stand there.

The guys dance out of the way of her swiping claws. "You filthy bitch!"

But for all their words, they're the ones who back up.

She watches them go, tail switching, flicking, lip curling over her fangs. She tracks me then, sees me standing there, watching. And her hackles rise again.

My bones unlock, and I hurry around the corner, out of sight. I can't take on anyone else's problems right now. I can't. Papá, Pilar, and what's left of me—it's already too much.

"How was school?"

Pilar sighs. I know I sound stupid, but it's what Mamá would have asked.

"We're studying butterflies."

I should say something about chrysalises. Or wings. Or caterpillars. But nothing comes out.

Great talk, Francisco.

I take her backpack and her hand, and we walk the rest of the way in silence. What is there to say anyway? We're stuck in our own husks of emotion, unable to break through, afraid of the struggle to drag our bloated wings from their prison.

When we walk into the prison courtyard, the disappointment on Papá's face is like a day-old sunburn, peeling skin away from skin, leaving an itchy, raw place behind.

"I told you, I'm not going." I don't know why he wastes his hope on something that's never going to happen.

But it's like he refuses to hear me. That night while he peels potatoes and stirs the pot of rice on the hot plate, he begins teaching us how to speak Aymara. Just a word here and there. *Willka*: sun. *Kurumi*: rainbow. *Jawira*: river.

I don't even pretend to try.

Pilar does, though. Papá has been slowly drawing her out, and she's talking more now—not chattering every second of the day like she used to, but the shock is draining from her eyes, and little by little, she's coming back to us.

So she practices the new words while she decorates our little cell with the things she finds on the street. Nothing wants to stick to the walls—nothing wants to be stuck in here—but she just picks the scattered things off the floor and tacks them back up again, with bits of reused tape, every time they fall. Moth wings separated from their bodies. A cracked cherry pit. Leaves with holes like lace punched through their desiccated skin.

It all looks like trash to me.

October 20

n the morning, I sling my backpack over my shoulder and follow Papá and Pilar out of our cell. I'm trying to put my finger on what it is that's different about Papá. I mean, he's sad, but who wouldn't be? He's underfed and uncomfortable and overworked, but so is everybody else in here.

Papá walks us through the dim hallway lined with cell doors stacked on top of each other like bats under a bridge. We go down the stairs, and through the courtyard. His arm is draped over Pilar's shoulders, and he's speaking softly over her head.

From this angle, you can't tell that something is seriously wrong. I don't see it until he turns and beckons to me, places my hand in my sister's, pats my cheek, and looks up into my face.

It's his eyes. You could see it before—the mind behind those eyes. And the heart too.

Now it's all I can do not to flinch when his eyes meet mine. They've dimmed and darkened, like whatever lit them from within is slowly being smothered.

"**Y**our homework," Profesor Perez says. A chorus of groans fills the classroom, and he holds up a hand. "I was only going to make it a five-paragraph essay. Should I make it seven?"

The groans stop.

"All right, then. A five-paragraph paper on the educational system in this country."

The bell clangs and the room fills with the shush and crumple of notebooks closing, and books sliding inside backpacks. The groans are back, too.

Reynaldo's seat is empty—I haven't seen him in a few days. My classmates push in their chairs and bodies bump down the aisle, out the door and into the outdoor patio at the center of the school.

"Francisco, a word?" Profesor Perez says.

Great.

"I have spoken to the rest of your teachers, and we are all concerned about you."

Here it comes.

"You have always gotten by on a minimum of effort."

I look up, sideways a little.

Profesor Perez's eyebrows rise halfway up his forehead. "Don't look so surprised. Of course we noticed. Now, I know things have become difficult for your family, but your performance at school has slipped. You're missing class, and even when you're here, you're not paying attention. You've been walking the edge for so long you might not realize how easy it is to slip off."

I lean my head back so maybe he can't see me roll my eyes.

"Did you know that only one in five teenagers finishes secondary school? If you don't get it together, after all these years of school, you won't receive a diploma. If you don't get a diploma, university is out of the question."

He looks at me like he expects a response, but what do I have to say? That I wish I wasn't even here? That school is the last thing on my mind right now? That there's no way I'm ever going to university?

"Francisco, do you have any idea how much potential you have?"

"You sound like my father."

"Well, your father sounds like a smart man. Francisco, this is serious. With only a few weeks of classes left, you can't give up now."

Great. The minute Papá stops riding me about school, my teachers start. How any of them think school matters one bit now that my life is walled in and locked up is beyond me.

I don't plan to follow the girl from the prison again after school, but my feet carry me that way anyway. Those guys are back. They don't stop her, don't try to touch her again, but they trail a step behind, baiting, laying steel jaws in the ground at her feet.

And I understand—finally—why Papá's pleas are so earnest. It's not just the one awful day Pilar already survived. It's years and years of days like that—and like this—after I leave. Guys like Red Tito in the prison, and guys like these on the streets.

Pilar will never be safe. I'll have to leave the prison in December when I turn eighteen, and without me, the wildcat life is all she will have. My sister is smart, but she doesn't have claws hiding beneath her skin.

I hurry to pick up Pilar. I'm not going to the Altiplano, no matter what Papá wants. But if I can't find another place for us to stay before I turn eighteen, we'll have no choice. Pilar will have to go.

October 21

W e don't get much class time to work on our essays, and we have only four weeks left until the end of school, so when Profesor Perez quits lecturing fifteen minutes before the bell on Thursday, the room is almost silent. I'm trying to get it down, everything I've learned about equity and education. But every time I try to write it out, it just ends up a mess of frustration and anger fighting for space on the page.

This is a research paper. It's not supposed to be emotional. But this isn't just an essay I have to get done to finish school. This is my life I'm writing about. It's my father's life on this page.

The Tránsito officer said Papá needs a lawyer. Well, we can't afford one. We can't afford it because he had access to only a couple of years of school. So what—he's stuck in prison forever? If he'd been the one with a chance to graduate secondary school, he would have made the most of it.

No matter how I perform the ablutions, the bead-by-bead recitations, it won't ever be enough. I could climb the steps to the Cristo every day on my knees, and still I'd never be half the man my father is.

If Papá had a diploma, he would have gone to university, for sure. Maybe not for poetry—he had to pay the bills, after all—but he could have been a teacher, or an engineer, or maybe even a lawyer.

And it all comes together, like boulders dislodged in a rockslide tumbling to the ground. Someone at the university should know about the 1008, or how to get a lawyer, or how to help us.

It's something, finally. Something I can do.

Profesor Perez stops me again, and I step out of the stream of students rushing for the door. The other students bump and press past me, jeering at my bad luck.

"Francisco, where's Reynaldo? He hasn't been at school all week."

I shrug. "I don't know, Profesor."

"And what about you—have you thought about what I said?"

I shrug for a second time.

Profesor Perez starts muttering under his breath, and I take the chance to slip out the door.

drag Pilar with me to Reynaldo's after school. The university will have to wait until tomorrow, even if I have to cut class to get there.

I ring the bell at the gate, but nobody comes outside. Pilar sticks her head between the bars, and the steel rods dig into her collarbone. We're just down the street from our old house, but she doesn't mention it, so neither do I. I don't want to know who lives there now, who dreams in my bed.

Whoever it is better know normal is no guarantee.

We wait for an hour or so—on the dirt in front of Reynaldo's house is as good as any place to kill time. But nobody comes, so we start the long walk back to the prison.

We pass the market on the corner with ads covering the whole awning, where Rey and I would always stop in for a Coke, thirsty and sweaty after playing fútbol all afternoon. The electric poles that line the street string dozens of wires between them, and they drape shadows like tiered necklaces on the walls behind.

We pass the pharmacy where I'd have to run in the evenings to buy a roll of chalky pills after Papá put too much pepper in his soup. He did it every time, no matter how much Mamá scolded him, and every time, he paid for it.

I've done this before, walked through the streets that used to be ours and rounded haunted corners thick with memory, but Pilar hasn't. She hasn't even asked to go back since that first day after Mamá left, and I went home without her. Nothing I say now will make it any better. And I can tell in the way

Pilar's whole face seems to sag—weighed down by things a kid shouldn't have to see, or try to understand—she's haunted by the ghosts of our old life too.

The last time she was here, life was this whole other thing, with good days and not-so-good days. But even on the bad days, another good day was just a sleep or two away.

It's the biggest thing prison has taken from me—from us: the idea that there's something good waiting just around the corner.

The cars that whiz by us don't care that Pilar's tired, that her head has begun to droop and her shoes scuff against the concrete. A stray dog lopes back the way we came, his head low to the ground, sniffing.

I see a figure duck around the corner, and I think maybe it's her—that girl from school. But what would I do if it was? She probably thinks I'm just another one of *them*.

We pass food carts made up of a tower of stacked crates and plastic coolers. Without meaning to, I turn my head away and hold my breath as we walk past. It's not seeing the food that gets to me. It's the smells.

They make me think of Mamá. They make me ask myself if things would have been different if I had even tried, just once, to make Mamá's burden a little lighter. They make me miss her, dammit.

Mamá hated cooking, and she wasn't very good at it. Her own mother had never cooked a day in her life. And I think Mamá always hated that after a long day at work she only had more work to do at home. So now, roasting meat smells like resentment, potatoes simmering in a stew of peppers and garlic are like missed opportunities, and chicken marrow broth is bitter as wasted dreams.

When we finally get back, I sit on the sun-warmed courtyard steps while Papá and Pilar buy some pork for tonight's soup.

The prison is crumbling all around us. The cracking plaster and ancient bricks die a little more each day, and the rubble sifts down the walls to the courtyard floor. Pebbles. Chipped paint. Bits of brick crushed underfoot. Someday the whole place is going to come crashing down on top of us. I roll the grit beneath my shoe in rough circles, around and around and around.

I take Pilar by the hand, climb the stairs to the second floor, and lock us in our cell. I grab my notebook and lean into the corner. We used to have our own room, just the two of us, and Pilar was always in my business. Now, with nothing to divide the space and not even a shred of privacy, she gets it. She turns the other way and leaves me to my thoughts.

It takes a few stops and starts, but I get them down on the page.

> *All my life*
> *I've been surrounded by walls.*
> *Over my head*
> *no matter how tall I grew,*
> *topped with sharp wire*
> *or shards of glass*
> *so no one would ever think of climbing them.*
>
> *At school, a wall around the grounds.*
> *At home, a wall around the yard.*
> *In town, a wall around every building.*

I never thought twice about it
until I found myself inside of walls meant
to keep people in.
Not to keep us safe,
but to hold us
trapped inside this unsafe place.

Now all I want is to tear down
the walls I have leaned on
all my life.

They're still there—these thoughts that have been banging around in my head like a fly trapped in a jar. But they're quieter now.

Papá comes inside after the prisoner count. Shadows rim his eye sockets.

The mattress is our bed and our couch and our dinner table. The three of us sit in a row facing the last of the light that comes in through the open doorway. All evening, the ghosts of my old life have been hanging over my shoulders and whispering in my ears.

I keep stopping and starting the same dense article about educational systems in South America and getting nowhere. I give the rice one last stir and unplug the hot plate from the outlet that hangs from a wire sticking out of a hole in the ceiling. Pilar hands me the bowls one by one, and I spoon out our dinner.

"Have a seat, Papá," I say as I stick a spoon in his bowl and give it to him. "Eat."

I pass Pilar her bowl. "Well, are you going to tell him?"

Pilar sets her dinner aside and clasps her hands in front of her, scooting on her knees until she's right next to Papá. "In December, before Francisco's birthday on the seventh, he's going to take me to live with Abuela and Abuelo." Pilar lifts the spoon to her lips and blows. "But not before, Papá."

Papá looks between the two of us and opens his mouth to speak, but Pilar raises a hand to stop him. "That's the deal. We get to stay with you a while longer. And then I will go. I don't want to, but I'll do it for you."

Pilar leans over and kisses Papá on the cheek. "I will write you a letter every day. And you will write me a poem every week."

Papá smiles. "Okay, *wawitay*. We'll make it work somehow

until then." He returns Pilar's kiss and then he leans across her to grip my shoulder. He waits until I meet his eyes. "And you?"

"Someone has to stay in the city, to check on you, Papá."

"I don't want you throwing away your life for me, Francisco."

My life? That's over. Even if the things I wanted and the way things were before was even still possible, I couldn't just go off and live my life while Papá is stuck in prison. I couldn't do that.

Maybe I'm not as much like Mamá as I thought.

October 22

In the morning, after I drop off Pilar at school, I go straight to the university. After all those nights wishing I knew what to do, it's like, now that my feet are actually moving in the direction of something that might make a difference, I can't get there fast enough.

The campus is surrounded by a chain-link fence with barbed wire at the top, and I run halfway around the place before I find an entrance. I find the law building easily enough, but the only person there is a first-year student who barely knows more than me.

"Maybe try the library?" he says with a shrug.

So I head that way, though I don't really know how a library will help get me a lawyer. I walk up to the clerk at the front desk. He's probably going to laugh me out of the place, but what do I have to lose?

"Excuse me. I need help finding a lawyer."

He nods. Maybe it wasn't such a ridiculous question after all. "The law books are right over there."

I walk over to the stacks he pointed out, and I'm about to go back to the front desk and explain that no—I don't need to read about the law, I need a lawyer to represent Papá. But then I notice the volumes are organized numerically.

I draw my finger along the spines: *500–510, 950–960, 1000–1010.* I flip through the pages until I find the 1008, and the text of the law that put Papá in prison. I read the whole thing, along with some commentary at the end. I read it twice. Three times.

None of it makes any sense. Big words in long sentences that don't actually say anything. *Narco-trafficking. Recidivism. Crop eradication. Pretrial detention.* I don't know what any of it means, but I copy it all down, word for word.

That night, Papá, Pilar, and I sit in a circle on the mattress.

He says, "I stopped chewing coca when I moved down from the Altiplano as a young man. It was a way of ending one life and beginning another."

Papá opens a plastic bag stuffed with dried coca leaves and dumps a pile on the blanket. "I think you know, coca is not a drug. It's like coffee—a little stimulant, that's all. You shouldn't be afraid of it. It is not a crime to honor your culture, even if the law books disagree. In my parents' community, coca is a sacred leaf. Chewing coca ties you to those around you and to Pachamama—the earth mother who sustains all life.

"When you meet your abuelos, they will present you with coca leaves. In doing this, they are offering you nothing less than admittance into their community, their *ayllu*." He ruffles Pilar's hair. "Of course, they probably won't give you any, *wawitay*, since you're so young."

Pilar screws up her face. "That's okay. I don't really want to eat a bunch of leaves anyway."

Papá laughs, and I lean in to whisper in my sister's ear, "Lucky you."

Papá pretends not to hear me. "Francisco, when you accept the coca leaves, you must make an offering in return. Like this." He takes three leaves and pinches them between his fingers. "Then you blow over them and say a blessing. Here, you try it."

This is the kind of thing all my ex-friends would scoff at,

something that would make me less in their eyes. But screw them. They're not my friends anymore anyway.

Besides, Papá is here like he hasn't been *here* in days. So I listen, and I repeat the Aymara words over and over until I can do it right.

October 23

On Saturday, Papá brushes the sawdust from his clothes and makes us breakfast. He helps us with our homework like he used to, checking answers and talking us through the ones we missed.

His hands have become callused. His palms are rough when he pats the back of my hand. This place is leathering him.

I shower, comb my hair, and dress in the cleanest clothes I have. I wipe the scuffs from my shoes and tell Papá I'm going to visit a friend. It would be easier if I could run all the way there, but I make myself go slowly so I don't work up a sweat.

When you're begging rich people for favors, you want to look your best. That way, even if they kick you to the curb, you can leave with dignity.

Mamá was always too proud to ask for help, but I don't see what else I can do. I walk up to the front door of a lawyer's office down the street from the bank where she used to work.

A bell dings as I open the door and walk inside. The receptionist looks me up and down. She doesn't smile.

"Yes?"

"I would like to meet with the lawyer, please."

She purses her lips. "And how will you be paying for the initial consultation?"

I swallow, and I make myself meet her eyes. "I am strong. I'm a quick learner. I can work off any fees he charges."

The receptionist inspects a manicured nail, then goes back to the paper in front of her. "Impossible. Come back when you can pay for the service you are requesting."

"Please, Señora, I will do anything."

She doesn't even look up at me again. "Waste one more minute of my time, and I'll call the police."

I back out of the office. Pointless. Why did I even bother?

The night is hot. Too hot to talk. Too hot to move.

Sweat slicks Papá's hair to his head and slides down his jawline. I watch while he soaks his hands in a bowl of water to coax the splinters from his skin.

I lie back on the mattress and stare at the ceiling, following the cracks in the plaster from floor to ceiling and back again. I stare so long my eyes blur, and the cracks seem to run with sweat, too.

October 24

S unday afternoon, Pilar tapes a helicopter seed (only split open and missing its seed) to the wall. While Papá sleeps, I pull out my copy of the 1008 and read it again. What do I know about coca or cocaine or how laws work? Nothing.

So what makes me think I could possibly help?

But I keep reading, mostly to understand why the police can put someone in prison before they know for sure he's guilty. I mean, I know life is rough out there. I know I have to keep my fists ready, because something or someone is always coming at me.

It just never occurred to me that it was the law that made it that way.

October 25

n writing class on Monday morning, I can't seem to focus
on anything. Besides, I'm not going to write a stupid love
poem. I'm not going to go on and on about a flower petal,
or sparkling sunlight or some shit. There's nothing sparkling
in my life right now. So I stop and I start again, only to drop
my pencil for good without getting down a single word.

Everybody around me seems to be having no problem
with Profesora Ortiz's assignment. Pour anything you think
and everything you feel onto the page. Like it's so easy. I look
around, and they're doing it—shaping ideas into stanzas. I
glance to the back row where the girl from the prison hunches
over her paper.

She looks up, and I look away.

I don't want to know what she thinks of me.

But I can't get her out of my head. I can't shake how I just
stood there when she needed help.

When the last bell of the day rings, I wait for her, my hands
clasped behind my back and my weight shifting from one foot

to the other. She bangs through the front doors, and I step in front of her.

Her cat eyes narrow to slits.

"I fell asleep in writing class." This was a stupid idea. I should just forget it. "Can I copy your notes?"

"I don't take notes." She keeps walking.

I jog to catch up and stay a full stride to her right so I can jump out of the way if she swipes at me. "Come on, just tell me what I missed?"

There is no way she'll go for this.

But after a moment, she starts talking about the lesson, and she doesn't stop me from walking beside her. A block away from school, we pass those same guys on the corner. I can feel their eyes like smacks against the back of my head. I'm glad she's the one talking, because my mouth is dry and my heart is banging against my chest like I just finished a full-field sprint.

They watch us walk past, and they don't fall in behind. They don't leer at her. They don't jump me. A few streets down, she stops walking, stops talking, and slides her gaze to the empty sidewalk behind us.

She looks at me then, for the first time. Her eyes are dark and set into round cheeks, her hair a round black line around her face. Everything is round, except her mouth. It's a flat line, turning down at the edges like she's still deciding how to deal with me.

"I'm Soledad."

I don't know what she's giving me here, but I feel it settle over my shoulders and warm the back of my neck.

"Francisco."

"You live at San Sebastián."

I nod.

The sun glances off her hair, like a ribbon of light sliding around her head whenever she moves. She wears her hair in braids and even ties yarn into the ends like a cholita. None of the other girls at school does that. Not one.

"I have to go get my sister now." I step into the street, stuff my hands in my pockets, and nod my head toward the primary school at the end of the block. Those cojudos are out of sight, so she doesn't have any reason to walk with me anymore.

But she steps into the street, too, and waits with me while I wait.

When the bell rings and the doors to the primary school fly open, a herd of noisy children stumble out. Soledad shifts a quarter turn in my direction. "San Sebastián is a shit place for you to live, I know. But for your sister? It's dangerous. If you have anywhere else you can go, you should leave, as soon as you can. If I had anywhere else—*anywhere* else to go, I would never set foot in that prison again."

I don't have time to explain, and anyway I don't want to talk about Mamá leaving, or about everything I can't do for Papá, and risk shedding more of whatever sinew is still holding me upright. I'm not ready for this girl to see me like that. So I just shift a quarter turn in her direction. And that's all the answer I can give, for now.

I don't know what Pilar reads into any of it, but after she's crossed the street, my sister moves into the space between Soledad and me. She takes my hand and pauses for a second, then reaches up to take Soledad's, too.

October 26

'm in history class working on the rough draft of my essay, and every question just seems to lead to another question to another unsatisfying answer. The only thing I really know is that us poor kids—we're set up to fail. From the start.

It's people with university degrees who make all the decisions—lawyers, judges, politicians. If you don't graduate from secondary school, no way are you going to university. If you live in a poor town, you don't even have a secondary school to go to. So what, then? Your chance of making it in the world is over before you even begin?

I stand, and my chair makes this loud scraping noise. Everyone is staring at me. I crumple all the stuttering starts of my essay into a ball and throw them into the trash can on my way out. Profesor Perez lets me go, even though there are still ten minutes left in class.

I wait for Soledad after school, and we walk together to get Pilar. I wish I knew how Soledad ended up like this. I mean, we've gone to the same school all our lives, but we're basically strangers.

I have algebra homework and a geography test to study for, but I don't really want to work on either. While we walk, I look over my notes from writing class. "I didn't get what Profesora Ortiz was saying about iambs and dactyls. Did you?"

"No, I wasn't paying attention."

"You're not going to do the poems?"

"I'm doing the assignment, I'm just not writing poems."

"What? How did you swing that?"

"I'm writing down the songs my abuela used to sing to me."

"Lucky."

Soledad rolls her eyes. "Well, I have to piece together the songs from memories that are mostly gone. I was just a kid when she died. And then I have to translate them from the original Aymara. And somehow, in the translation, I have to make the new words sound like they've always belonged together."

Okay, so maybe her way isn't so easy either.

We stop in front of the primary school and lean into the shade of a flowering tree. Soledad scuffs her heel against the brick wall we're leaning against and turns to face me. "What are you writing about that you need to know all about those dactyls or whatever?"

"I don't know," I say. "Nothing good. Just life, I guess."

"Who gets to say what's good and what's not? If it's real, and if it's true, that sounds like poetry to me."

After we pick up Pilar, we head to the cancha, but I stop short of the tarp awnings. There's a policeman there, scanning the area. I may not understand the 1008, or anything really about the system that put Papá in prison, but it's the police who make the arrests, and the police who guard the prison. The least I can do is keep away from them when I can.

"Let's just walk a bit," I say.

"Sure—whatever." Soledad plays it off like it's no big deal, but her eyes track the officer as we veer around the corner.

In the middle of a run-down side street, Pilar stops walking, and I stop with her to see what she's looking at. It's the same broken little city through the archway that we passed a couple of weeks ago. Street kids are everywhere. It looks just as filthy as the prison.

"We should keep going," Soledad whispers.

"Why—what's wrong?" I ask.

"These places are bad. We need to leave." She's nervous. Her claws are ready, her tail lashing.

Pilar grips my hand and ducks behind my arm.

"But those kids are just like us, right? With nowhere else to go?"

She turns on me then. "I told you. If there was *anywhere* better than San Sebastián, I would go there."

I'm an idiot. It's one thing to be reckless with my words and my fists and myself. But not with her. And especially not with Pilar. "Okay, you're right. Let's go."

Footsteps scuff against the concrete behind me, and Soledad's eyes slide to the space just over my left shoulder. She tightens her hold on Pilar's hand.

"What are you doing here?"

I know that voice.

"Reynaldo?" I spin around. He's flanked by a pair of guys. Thick, tough guys.

"Who else?"

"Where have you been? Profesor Perez keeps asking why you're not in school."

He motions to the crumbling arch and the courtyard beyond. "Why would I bother with school when I have all this?"

"You live here now?"

"Mamá kicked me out. Where else was I supposed to go?" His arms drop back to his sides. And a little of the bravado drops off too.

"Your má kicked you out? Why?"

He leans in, whispering, "She found a stash of drugs in my room."

I knew he was dealing. But still, this catches me off guard. "So you live here, with these street kids?"

He lifts one shoulder in a shrug. "I almost have enough saved to get a place of my own. You could join us, Francisco. We can still open our shop. We can have it all."

For the first time, I don't have anything to say to Reynaldo. He told me it was temporary, that he was just doing what he had to so we could get our shop off the ground. There are hundreds of people stuck in San Sebastián because of drugs, and that's what Reynaldo wants with his life? Really?

I back away, pulling Pilar and Soledad with me. "I can't. Papá needs me. Pilar needs me."

"Yeah?" Reynaldo calls after me. "And what about you, Francisco? Who is looking out for you?"

Reynaldo's words hang over me the whole walk home, and through dinner, and while I toss and turn, trying to sleep.

Who is looking out for you?

He only asked what I would have asked before. *What about you, Rey? You've got to look out for you.*

The thing is, Papá was always looking out for me, and, as much as I hated it, pushing me to reach for more than the world offered. He's still looking out for me, in the little ways he can.

And, yeah, it's awful in here. But I can get out when I need to, when I need a breath, when I need to throw my head back and just let the sky swallow me.

Papá can't do that. And I don't know how to say to my friend who used to think like I thought and want what I wanted out of life, that everything is different now. He's different, and I'm different, and I don't know if I can go where he's headed.

I wake in the middle of the night in a cold sweat. I sit up, run my fingers through my hair, and rest my elbows against my knees, waiting for my breath to settle, for the panic to work its way out of my pores.

I close my eyes and the dream is right there, hovering at the edge of sleep. I see Reynaldo—not like he is now, but as a kid. As a six-year-old kid like the day we first met.

He's trying to hold his father's charango in his hands and play at the same time, but the round bowl keeps slipping against his stomach. He's singing a serenata for his mother, and the light is on inside the house, but she won't open the shutters.

Reynaldo is singing as loud as he can, but rivers and rivers of tears slide down his cheeks and fill his mouth to overflowing until he's choking and he can't sing anymore.

I blink myself awake, blink back the dream, all the time gasping for breath like it's me who's drowning.

October 27

Waking up from a bad dream is like waking up with a head cold. It feels like there are cotton balls packed around all the empty spaces in my brain.

I look for Soledad between classes. She's by the wall, alone.

"Hey," I say as I lean against the bricks a ways down from her. The street is empty. The school is quiet, for once. Even the wind is still. "How come I never see you doing homework?"

Soledad shrugs.

"You're not going to do the history essay?"

"No—I am," she says. "That one matters. I just don't need to spend hours in the library to write a paper on educational inequity and the movement for indigenous rights."

"Is that even a thing?"

She cuts her eyes sideways at me. "Funny."

"I'm sort of serious."

She looks at me like I've lost it. "Yeah, it's a thing. Have you ever seen an indigenous person in a government position? Or haven't you noticed that they don't teach the Quechua or Aymara languages in public schools? Think about it,

Francisco—who is filling the prisons? Not the light-skinned professional class. Us. We are. Don't tell me you've never been called a stupid *indio.*"

"I mean, people are jerks, but I didn't think anybody was doing anything about it. I didn't think there was anything we *could* do about it."

Soledad rolls her eyes, "Well, if you think like that, then there definitely won't be."

When the school day ends, I don't make up some stupid excuse, and I definitely don't try to start a conversation, I just stand to leave when Soledad does and fall in beside her.

She never said *don't touch me.* She didn't have to. I understood from the beginning that even if she's falling, even if I'm only trying to stop her from stepping in front of a speeding car, even if it's just to cushion her fall—if I touch her, it will break whatever not-quite-trust thing we have going.

We collect Pilar, and Soledad takes us to a food cart for lunch, then to a small biblioteca run by volunteers from the local police station. There are only a few dozen books on a single metal shelf, and you can't take any of them home with you. Can you really call it a library if it hardly has any books?

There are kids everywhere—huddled around the tables and sprawled on the floor. I don't recognize any of them from the prison, so maybe they're street kids? Or maybe they have families, and they're just waiting for their parents to get off work. I bet they don't have any idea how lucky they are.

I wish we could take a book back to the prison with us—it would give Pilar something to do after she finishes her homework besides playing with rocks and insect carcasses and her doll that's become as filthy as everything else in the prison. But for now at least, my sister is curled up in a mound of pillows by the window. All afternoon, she's like a regular kid—napping, flipping through a book, and staring out the window.

When I was in primary school, I spent every afternoon with Reynaldo, running all over the neighborhood. Lots of kids my age had to work after school, but Mamá had a good job. And she was proud. She came from an elite family where kids could be kids. Papá had worked from the time he was a little boy, and he didn't want that for us. Both of my parents wanted us to have a real childhood.

So what changed, Mamá?

You just gave up. Why?

It got too hard? You lost hope? What?

I pull out a pen and paper, and I hunch over the table so Soledad can't see. This time, I don't even think, I don't try to shape the lines or the ideas. I just let it go.

> *When I see my mother in my dreams*
> *she is the oldest woman in the world*
> *wrinkles like arroyos gouge her face.*
> *Her eyes are white as clouds.*
>
> *I am afraid of this anciana,*
> *this vision of my mother.*
> *Was she always so worn*
> *and I just couldn't see it?*
> *Was she always so tired?*
>
> *Every time, in the dream,*
> *the white drains out of her eyes,*
> *a flash flood that washes down her cheeks*
> *mud sloughing off*
> *until her face is smooth and young and bright*
> *her cheekbones high,*
> *her eyes uplifted.*
>
> *Is this what she was*
> *before she was a mother?*
> *Did I do this to her?*

The officer behind the desk gives Pilar candies. And he holds his hands behind his back when he speaks to Soledad. But when he looks at me, his smile falters.

Papá wouldn't be in prison if it weren't for the police. We wouldn't be motherless if Papá wasn't in prison. I don't say what I'm thinking, but I also don't lower my gaze. I let my eyes say what my voice doesn't, and I see in the way the edges of the officer's mouth fall downward when he looks at me that he hears it.

When we get back to the prison, the three of us walk up the stairs together, and Soledad stops at her cell door. She tugs on the chain around her neck, pulls out a key, and turns it in the lock.

"Do you want to come over after dinner?" Pilar asks.

Soledad shakes her head. She slips through the open door and closes it behind her before I can sort the shadows inside into shapes. The bolt scrapes, steel on steel, as the door locks again from the inside.

The prisoners have been counted for the night, the gates are shut, and Pilar and I are in our cell. Papá's in the shower washing himself and our laundry. I'm reading through my notes on the 1008 again, but it's not helping.

With the last of the light coming in from the small window, Pilar is drawing on the back of one of her school assignments. I should be doing my homework, but I can't bring myself to care.

What does any of it matter if I can't get Papá a lawyer?

If we were home, Mamá would be cooking over the stove and Papá would be at the table with Pilar and me, checking our work and asking us a million questions. I think he did that as much for himself as anything. He was the one who wanted to learn, not me.

I would always put up with it for a while—just long enough to keep him off my back. Then, as soon as I could after dinner, I'd get out of there and go to Reynaldo's while Mamá and Papá and Pilar spent the rest of the evening together.

Maybe Pilar did this sort of thing then, too? Maybe she drew pictures for Papá in answer to his poems or to remind Mamá of us while she was at work all day, and I was just never around to notice?

I can see it now—Pilar lying on her belly on the carpet, kicking her heels together in the air as the heavy curtains over the window let in a muted light. Papá and Mamá sitting together on the couch, not at opposite ends like normal adults, but squeezed together on the same cushion and talking in soft tones.

Why was I in such a hurry to get away from that?

Here there's no soft carpet for Pilar to lie on. She's sitting on the far corner of the mattress, turned away from me.

"What are you drawing?"

Pilar's head lifts away from the wall, and she turns to look at me. A small line forms between her eyebrows. "A feather."

I scoot over and look at the pencil drawing on the gravel-pocked paper. "It's nice."

The line disappears, and Pilar tilts her head to the side. "I think it looks like a smile, don't you?"

"I guess I could see that."

"It's for Soledad. I think she might be lonely at night."

Pilar's hand is steady, but the ground the paper rests on isn't anything close to smooth, so the plumes come out all crooked. The thing looks bent and wiggly at the edges, but it's kind of perfect that way.

I thought it was a good thing that I was tough, that I wouldn't back down from a fight. I thought it would help us survive in this place. But I'm beginning to wonder if Pilar's way is better. Just a solid grip on the good things—any good things you can find.

When Papá comes back, his hair wet but clean and our damp clothes hanging over his arms, I walk with Pilar to Soledad's cell. My sister bends down and scoots the paper under the gap at the bottom of the door until just a sliver of white is visible. We hear a shuffling sound from inside and the paper is whisked away, out of sight.

We walk back to our cell, lock ourselves inside, and help Papá hang up the clothes so they'll dry by morning. Pilar smiles only once, just a little, to herself. But somehow it fills the place up all night.

October 28

Papá is not writing.

He hasn't written a single poem since he came to San Sebastián. I wonder what his mind is like with all those thoughts churning around, stuck in there.

His poems were how we always talked about things. I mean—we argued about school, and we chatted about fútbol matches. But real things? Like the kind of man he wanted me to be? Like how much he loved me? That was harder to say face-to-face. We talked about those things through his poems.

Okay, so that was pretty much a one-way conversation for the last few years.

Maybe it's time for me to answer.

Profesora Ortiz says that Pablo Neruda wrote his poems in green ink because it's the color of hope. Maybe that's what Papá needs to start writing again—a little hope. So today in class, when I'm supposed to be filling in a grammar work-sheet on irregular verbs in the present subjunctive or some shit, I borrow a lime green pencil from the girl behind me and start copying down one of Federico García Lorca's poems, "Hora de Estrellas." There's this part about being ripe with lost poetry, and I think maybe that's how Papá feels.

I'm halfway done when Profesora Ortiz catches me. She lifts the page and adjusts her reading glasses while her lips move soundlessly.

"I've always loved that one," she whispers, and she sets the paper back down on my desk, covering it with the grammar worksheet. She taps her finger beside the still-empty spaces waiting for answers.

I'll finish the poem later, maybe in the hall between classes. Then, I'll hide it for Papá to find, just like he used to do for me.

After school, I have the whole table at the biblioteca to myself. Soledad is helping Pilar with her math homework in the pile of pillows by the window. I pull my copy of the 1008 out of my bag and read it through. I still don't get it.

"Can I help you?" The officer leans over my shoulder.

"I doubt it."

"Suit yourself. But I do know a thing or two about that law. I could save you some time."

I close my eyes. Fold my paper in half. I don't want any favors from him, from one of *them*. But I'm not finding the real story on my own. I'm not getting it.

"*Fine.*"

"May I sit?" I don't say no, so he drags a chair over and sits facing me. His tag says TORRES. His eyes say he's used to being hated by kids like me.

He takes a deep breath, like we're going to be here awhile. "Parts of the story everyone knows: coca, a plant that has been grown and harvested for centuries without breeding addiction and crime and drug dealers, was turned into cocaine. A couple of decades ago, it exploded onto the international drug market. A drug like that is a big problem. It ruins lives. It destroys entire countries."

Officer Torres sighs and runs his fingers through his thinning hair. "What people don't understand is why coca became the enemy. You see, we take so much money in aid from the U.S.—when they say jump, our government jumps, even if it's over a cliff. They demanded drug arrests. They threatened economic sanctions and funded military action. Their president needed a win in his unwinnable war on drugs. So they pressured our government to draft la Ley del Régimen de la Coca y Sustancias Controladas—the 1008—to find and imprison people with any connection to coca—no matter that the law violated citizens' rights protected by our constitution."

I take notes while he's talking, like I'm in class or something.

"But do you think we caught the real drug dealers with this law? No. We caught the peasants who grew coca to ease the pain of dust from the mines in their lungs. We caught people who were in the wrong place at the wrong time, or who did something stupid just once, to make a little money to pull themselves out of bitter poverty."

And taxi drivers who just needed some gas so they could drive home to their families?

"The worst thing about the 1008 wasn't the arrests, though. It was the sheer number of them flooding the courts. Sure, we filled the prisons, but did those people get a sentence, or a trial, or a chance to defend themselves?"

I keep writing, and he answers his own question.

"No." He rubs his thumb against the stubble on his chin. "Not nearly enough of them. So what are we going to do about this? Blame the police? Blame the gringos? Blame our government? Okay—fine. But what good will any of that do? They're working to amend the unconstitutional parts of the law, but the prisons are still full of people whose only crime is being too poor to afford a lawyer."

Tell me about it.

But even if they emptied the prisons today of everyone like Papá who never did anything wrong—even if they could do that—they still couldn't make it right. Are they going to give Papá back his dignity? What about his livelihood? Are they going to bring Mamá home? Are they going to put Pilar back together?

So, yeah, I blame the police, and the gringos, and the government. All of them.

look for José before the prisoner count, while Papá is with Pilar, and find him in his family's cell. They're all sitting on the bottom bunk, listening while their father reads out loud from an open book in his hands.

When he sees me, José drops his arms from around his brothers' shoulders and scoots off the bed. Out on the balcony, he leans against the railing and turns his face to where the sun is just barely visible above the roofline.

"Hey," I say, and he nods. "Look, I know you don't have any reason to help me out, but I've been thinking about what you said last week—about the 1008. I looked it up in the library at San Simón, but that didn't really help. This policeman tried to explain it to me today, but nothing he has to say does me any good. I thought since you—"

José kicks away from the railing. "Hang on." He ducks back into his cell and comes out a few minutes later holding a small piece of paper with an address printed on the faded blue lines.

"Look, don't get mad, I'm just telling you like it is. You'll have years while your papá is stuck in here to learn about that stupid law. But first, there's something you should do." He hands me the paper. "This is the address of a legal aid society that takes the cases of people who are innocent. They don't charge for their services, and the sooner your papá's name is on their list, the sooner he might get out of here."

I hold the scrap of paper in both of my hands. Such a small thing to bear so much weight. "José—" I swallow, and try again. "I don't deserve—"

"It's okay."

I tuck the paper into my shirt pocket and press my hand over it, over my heart.

"This place can bring out the worst in people. If that was the worst you've got, you're going to be okay," José says.

He sounds so sure.

October 29

When we leave school on Friday, Soledad doesn't go with me to get Pilar.

"There's something I have to do," she says. She won't meet my eyes. "I'll see you." She walks away, and I'm alone on the sidewalk, watching the spot where she disappeared around the corner.

I pick up Pilar, tuck her backpack into my own, and pretend I don't notice the disappointment on her face when she sees it's just me. I take her hand, and we walk across town to the address José gave me for legal aid.

I try to focus on this—a chance for us after all this time. A lawyer for Papá.

I'm used to anger. And frustration. And disappointment. But hope? I don't know how to walk around with hope infecting everything I touch and see and breathe.

Inside the legal aid office, two women sit behind cluttered wooden desks, clattering away on plastic keyboards, the light from their computer screens casting a purple glow on their skin. The chairs at the entrance are full of people waiting their turn.

None of us make eye contact. It's like, maybe if that woman with the baby drooling all over everything gets a lawyer to hear her case, then Papá won't. What kind of cojudo wants to cut in line ahead of a baby?

Me. I do.

The hours creep by. I watch the clock hands tick in lazy circles against a wall the years have stained an ugly beige.

Two o'clock. Cobwebs stretch from the fake brass rim of the clock to the ceiling.

Three thirty. Frustration simmers under my skin.

Five o'clock. We have to be back at the prison by six, or we'll be locked out for the night. Papá will never forgive me if I don't get Pilar back in time.

Besides, we haven't had anything to eat since breakfast. I stand and pull Pilar up with me. One of the women calls out to us, without taking her eyes off her computer screen, "Write your name here." She passes me a clipboard and a pencil. "We'll bump your name to the top of the list when you return on Monday."

I press too hard, and the pencil lead snaps. Still without looking, the woman pulls another pencil out of her hair and hands it to me. I write our names and push through the swinging door.

October 30

I t's Saturday, and Pilar is reading a story to Papá in our cell, the two of them hiding in the shadows from the heat. I can't just sit in the same little room all day. Not when I just want the weekend to be over already so I can get back to legal aid. Not when I finally have something to look forward to.

I walk along the balcony, my hand dragging on the railing, my steps slowing as I approach the door to Soledad's cell. Maybe she's sick of being shut in all day too.

The door is open, so I peer inside.

"Hello?"

A man sits on the bottom bunk. His head tilts a little at the sound of my voice, but he doesn't answer.

"Is Soledad here?" I ask, even though I can see she's not. Besides, if she were here, the door would be closed, and locked.

The man—it must be her father—just sits there. His eyes are vacant, his mouth hanging open a little, the fingers on his right hand twitching. I back away.

No wonder she spends every second she can away from this place.

spend the rest of the day in the law library, reading everything I can get my hands on: proposed amendments to the 1008, articles on prison overcrowding and revolts against living conditions.

When I get back to the prison later that afternoon, I drag my backpack out onto the balcony. It's better than being stuck in the cell, but even out here, I'm constantly reminded of the way the prison walls cut off the edges of the sky, like even the air, and the clouds, and the horizon are off-limits for us.

I should be studying for my math test on Monday, but my thoughts just keep sliding back to what Officer Torres said. I pull out the notes I took at the library and read them again. I'm not sure why I even bother—what could I possibly do to change any of this?

I'm about to shove everything back into my backpack when something catches my eye in the courtyard below. Red Tito is down there, looking up at the balcony. But he's not watching me. His eyes are on the open door to Soledad's cell.

October 31

On Sunday, while Pilar and Papá are down in the courtyard for Mass, I tuck my copy of García Lorca's poem under Papá's pillow.

We'll spend today scrubbing everything in our cell for Todos Santos tomorrow, to make a welcoming space for the dead. Maybe he'll find it then, and maybe he'll write me back.

For lunch, Papá heats a pot of rice and sliced yellow potatoes dusted with ají amarillo on the hot plate. He taps the spoon against the edge of the pot and sets out three bowls.

What if he'd stayed on the Altiplano? What if he had followed his father into the mines? Maybe he'd be free. Maybe he wouldn't be walking around with a cracked-open heart in his chest all day long.

I'd take ruined lungs over a busted heart any day.

The García Lorca poem is taped to the wall beside a pair of thin-veined butterfly wings. He doesn't say a word about it, though, so neither do I. Instead, we talk about the wood shop, about Pilar's new friend Mariela at school, and the experiment we did in science class last week.

I don't tell Papá that I may have finally found a way to get him a lawyer, that I think we might get out of here someday soon. That maybe we can even move back into our old home, where we can eat like a family around a table and sleep without breathing air damp with pent-up frustration. That we might be able to hike together up to the hills surrounding the city and take in the whole sky, from horizon to horizon, with no walls and no wire and no guards with guns cutting off our view.

It's like the sting of fresh garlic in my mouth, this taste of hope. I swallow it down and swallow it down, but it keeps rising back up.

November 1

Monday morning, when Soledad falls into step beside Pilar and me, relief is like a bucket of water dumped over my head and washing over my skin. I try to play it off like I didn't notice she was gone, like I didn't care.

But she knows—I can tell. The air between us is different. Charged, somehow. And it's no good pretending otherwise.

rofesora Ortiz talks about rhythm and repetition in poetry and then she sits behind her desk like ten minutes of instruction is supposed to turn us into geniuses. I was thinking I'd write about soccer—that's got rhythm. But the scary thing about writing poems is sometimes things come out on the page that you'd never admit to even thinking.

> If I were Pablo Neruda
> (that horny bastard)
> I would go on and on about your black hair
> your golden skin,
> your ruby red lips
> (though they're more like the earth, really,
> like the dirt when it's been splashed by water—
> that rusty brown
> of wet earth).
>
> But when I think of you,
> what a poem about you
> should be,
> I see the wild thing inside of you
> the fur
> the claws
> the fangs.
> Do I have to make peace with the animal
> before I can see the girl?
> How could I ever even think

of kissing those wet earth lips
(which I really want to do)
((really))
when they hide fangs
underneath?

There's no way I'll ever show Soledad. I'll probably never even turn it in to Profesora Ortiz. Way too embarrassing. I don't even know why I wrote it.

After school gets out, we head straight to legal aid. Soledad comes with us this time, though she stops short of the stucco high-rise, sits on a concrete planter out front, and leans back against the trunk of a young palm tree. She looks calm enough, but even though her head is tipped back, she doesn't close her eyes, not fully. She keeps them open, in slits, so she can see trouble coming before it gets to her.

"Come in with us," I offer.

"That's okay."

"Did you already go through all this for your father?"

"My father wasn't innocent."

"Oh." I yank the door open, but turn back before I walk through. "It's safer inside. You could—"

"Francisco, I survived out here alone for years before you came along. I can take care of myself for a few hours."

I can't seem to get it right, not with her. If I could just say what I actually mean—that I want her there by my side—things might go better for me. But I can't say those kinds of things.

Not the vulnerable things.

Not the truth.

Inside, we only have to wait for one person to finish before the woman with the pencils stuck into her hair calls my name.

Pilar drops into the empty chair and I scoot mine up to the desk. I tell the woman about Papá, how he hasn't been sentenced yet and still has no trial date. I tell her how he was just a taxi driver, and not involved at all with cocaine.

She peers over her glasses at us. "Don't take this the wrong way, but are you sure?"

"Of course I'm sure. He is one hundred percent innocent."

"Yes, well, we like to be certain. Our resources are extremely limited." She pushes her reading glasses up her nose. "Take these forms and have your father fill them out. Drop them off later this week, and we'll begin processing them."

She hands me the papers, and I try to quit grinning like an idiot, but it's just—I almost can't believe this is finally happening for us.

The woman purses her lips like something sour has worked its way into her mouth. "You children need to realize that this is not a quick process. We will file a protest right away. It is best to file quickly after incarceration, and to show a series of inquiries and appeals. It causes the judge to look more favorably on the case when it finally comes before him."

"And we came in soon enough—it's not too late for Papá?"

She puts up a hand. "No, no, you're fine." But then she sighs, and I see it's coming now. The sour-tasting thing. "But the waiting list for one of our team of lawyers to try your father's case is three years out."

My head goes fuzzy. A ringing sound bounces back and forth between my ears. "But I turn eighteen in December. I'll have to leave the prison then. You want us to leave our father alone in there for three years?"

The woman ducks my eyes, but she keeps talking. She must give this same speech twenty times a day.

"The reality is, even if your father's case is heard by a judge three years from now, and if the judge rules favorably, the law mandates that every innocent verdict is followed by an appeal, and it will most likely be several more years before he is released. I am sorry. If we had more lawyers, we could do better, but they make no money from these cases. They have to earn a living too."

My fingers clench and the paper crumples. "So what do we do until then? No job I can get will pay enough to keep us off the street." I'm shouting now; I can't help it. "What do you expect us to do?"

"I can't help you with that, and there are others in line I must see to now. Speak with your father. Have him fill out the forms. Develop a plan as a family. And don't lose hope that your father will one day be free. It doesn't happen nearly as quickly or as often as it should, but it does happen."

Pilar must see that I'm worthless—stuck to my chair like a lump of flesh. She takes the papers, slides them into my backpack, and thanks the woman. Then she grabs my hand and pulls me up and out the door.

If Soledad sees it in our faces when we get outside, she doesn't pry. Maybe she never expected much to come of all this. I did, even though I should have known better.

Don't lose hope. What a joke. I could cover the whole world in green ink, and still there wouldn't be a speck of hope to be found.

t's late. Pilar is drawing and labeling some life cycle diagram. Birds maybe? Or bats? Papá is rolling a glinting gray rock the size of a fingernail around in his palm.

"What is that, Papá?" Pilar asks.

"This?" He holds it up to the light, and it winks at us. "This is fool's gold."

I don't like the way he says that.

"My father carried this little rock out of the mines and gave it to me when I left the Altiplano. Look, it's sparkly and yellow in places, like gold. But it's worthless."

"I never saw it before."

"Yeah, well, I forgot about it, for years." His lips twist from a grimace to an unconvincing smile. "Your mother packed it for me. She must have wanted me to have something of my father's while I'm here."

Pilar nods, matches his smile, and goes back to her drawing. But she's not stupid. She can see through those skin-deep smiles, same as me.

I grab my notebook and a pen and lie on my stomach, my pillow over my head so no one can see what I'm doing.

> *It looks like gold:*
> *yellow and shiny*
> *pried from the bottom of some*
> *dim mine shaft.*

It looks like a promising journey:
out of the hills
down to the city
into a new life.

It looks like a real marriage:
a house
two kids
a pair of decades together.

It looks like hope:
a trial
a verdict
the chance to be free again.

But it's only fool's gold.
All of it.

November 2

Sometimes going to school, we take the long way on purpose. I steer Pilar away from all the other prison kids and onto a side street. It takes longer, so after I tuck her doll into her backpack, smooth the flyaway hairs that have come loose since breakfast, and wait until she gets inside, I end up running with Soledad all the way to school just to get there before the first bell.

But it's worth it, to get a few minutes away from it all. To walk down a street that hasn't quite woken up yet. To pretend for a few minutes that life is normal, peaceful even, and that prison is the last place we belong.

Profesora Ortiz is calling us up one by one to privately go through the poems we have turned in so far. While I wait for my turn, I'm supposed to be writing a new one. I could write about how I never get the chance to play fútbol anymore, and how missing the thing that set the rhythm of my days is like skipping heartbeats. I could write about Pilar, or Papá. But all that's coming out is more about Soledad.

She sits a couple of seats behind me and to the left. The thought that she might somehow see what I'm writing makes heat spread like a rash over my neck and ears, but I don't stop. It's like I can't.

There is nothing smooth or tame about her.
She is tangles
and mats of fur
yowls that raise the hair on my neck,
and fangs.
I wonder, what does a wildcat want?
What would make
her tail swish against the floor?
What would loose a low rumble of pleasure
inside her chest?

When we get to the biblioteca after school, Pilar and Soledad curl up on the pillows by the window and I go straight to Officer Torres's desk. "Why don't they change the 1008, then, if everybody knows it's wrong?"

"Hello, there. Francisco, isn't it? I am so glad to see you here again."

I don't echo the greeting. I don't do the niceties.

He sighs. "Changing the law is not so easy. Why don't you have a seat?"

I sit on the edge of the wooden chair. I don't want to settle in with this guy.

"If you think the police are corrupt, you should spend a day in the halls of our government. They do what benefits them, more often than not. They do what is popular. They do what the wealthy ask of them. Is anyone of consequence banging down their doors and asking for prison reform? Are any of the elite calling their offices to protest the backlogged legal system?"

The whole time he's talking, his hands are clasped in front of him, his thumbs circling around each other in slow revolutions. How can he be so calm when this is my life he's talking about?

"Hey, I've got an idea. Why don't you do something about it, if you know so much? Stop the police from making pointless arrests. You're one of them. Make them stop."

"I could certainly try," Officer Torres says, nodding like he deserves everything I'm putting on him. "But who would be here in my place?" He sweeps his hand around the small room, at the children tucked into the corners and crowded around the tables. "We each serve where we are called. When I'm not at work, I'm volunteering here, so these kids have a safe place off the streets and away from the gangs and the pimps and the drug dealers. You think I should give that up?"

No. Obviously. But I'm not going to tell him that.

"What do we really need? Young people. Committed young people who will wade into the high waters and reroute this stream. People with the smarts to go to university. People with the energy and the motivation to fix this mess.

"Me? I do the best I can by this community. I enforce the laws of this country. If the laws need changing, well, I am not equipped for such a task." His hands clasp together again, and his thumbs resume their circling. "I wonder who might be?"

I hear the grunt I give in answer. I look over my shoulder. Pilar and Soledad are both watching me, like they can feel the tension rippling off my back. I can't help it. This guy makes me feel like my own skin is on too tight.

"Time to go, Pilar."

The three of us step out onto the dusty street, into the rusty almost-sunset sky that bleeds over the bricks and onto my burning cheeks.

When we walk past the guards and into the prison, the air in the place is different. The prisoners have set out extra plates for their ancestors, and the little stores around the courtyard sell tantawawas in the shape of swaddled infants and ladders so the souls of the dead can climb into the sky at the end of their visit.

There's no Día de los Muertos feast in prison, but while Papá and Pilar make dinner, he talks about his grandparents and his brother who died as a child as if they were right here with us.

I don't have space in my head for ghosts.

After dinner, I look over the notes I took at the law library. It's all jumbled on the page and tangled up in my head. It feels like the low ceiling of our cell is pressing down on me, and I don't know if it's because the dead are looking over my shoulder or if it's just the long, frustrating day, but I'm having trouble pulling in a full breath. I stare at the page in front of me, and the words seem to twitch and sway.

I rip out a second page and let the ideas reshape themselves.

> *People in another country,*
> *that big-stick-carrying country to the north,*
> *don't like what our coca leaf becomes*
> *when it is crushed and strained,*
> *crystallized and euthanized.*
> *They don't like how the tiny rocks pulverize*
> *the minds*

of pushers and prostitutes;
how all the money and power in the world still
can't keep their people clean.

They brought their big stick to our government,
they wrote quotas that have the prisons in this country
overflowing
with men and women waiting
for a sentence, hoping
for a trial, knowing
they'll never get it—

knowing they'll never again see
an uninterrupted view of the sky.

This one I'll turn in. I don't mind showing Profesora Ortiz angry. I let the whole world see that part of me.

We've been waiting a while for Papá to get back from the showers. Pilar looks like she's going to fall asleep sitting up, but she won't go to bed until we're all safe inside the cell for the night. Finally, the lock turns. Pilar rubs her eyes, and we both look up to see Papá sidle inside and quickly shut and lock the door behind him. His shoulders rise and then fall again, and he turns to face us.

His knuckles are bloody. His shirt is ripped. One eye is purple and swelling shut.

"Papá!" Pilar cries.

He motions for her to stay seated and sinks down to the mattress beside us.

I jump up. "What happened?"

"It's nothing."

"Papá!"

"Francisco," he whispers through bloodied lips, "sit."

Pilar grabs a washcloth and dabs at a line of blood by his ear. Papá tries to smile, but it doesn't work. He meets my gaze over Pilar's head. His eyes hold this dark thing I've never seen in my father before.

We're losing him.

November 3

I watch as Papá helps Pilar get ready for school. He's rubbing a scrap of cloth against a smudge on her shoe. His eyelids are barely open. The lines that shape his cheeks, the corners of his mouth, the squint of his eyes are all pitched down. Even his skin is tired of holding itself up.

This man is not my papá.

I can't wait the years it will take legal aid to get us out. There has to be another way. I pull my shoes on and lace them slowly, methodically. I've already started sweating along my hairline and beneath my button-down shirt. Yeah, it's hot. But this is something else.

This is me knowing what I have to do.

When I get to school, I let out a deep breath and open the door to Profesor Perez's classroom.

"Okay," I say. "What do I have to do?"

My teacher looks up from the stack of papers he's grading, his eyes blinking to bring me into focus. "To graduate? Turn in your assignments and prepare for the end-of-year exams in a few weeks. And come to class. Don't make me go down to the prison to tell your father you've been skipping school."

"No, not that." If I can't even say it, how am I ever going to make this work? "How do I get into the University of San Simón?"

Profesor Perez pulls off his reading glasses and motions for me to sit. "This is a surprise. What changed, Francisco?"

"Everything. And nothing. My father wants me to go with my sister up to my grandparents' home on the Altiplano. But that leaves Papá all alone just so we're safe. At what price?"

I sag onto the desk behind me. "I think prison is killing my father."

Profesor Perez leans forward, resting his forearms on the desk and steepling his fingers.

"It will be three years before Papá can get a trial. The people at legal aid said they could work faster if they weren't so understaffed. I couldn't help them now if I tried—I don't know enough. They need more lawyers or law clerks or something. They need educated people to help."

"So you want to become that person."

"It's the only way I can try to make any of this even a little bit okay. I can't just leave Papá in there without any hope."

By now the hallways are filling. Class is about to start. Profesor Perez taps his pen against the wooden desk.

"Will you help me?"

He drops his pen and stands. "Certainly." He leans forward, bracing his weight on his fingertips. "But, Francisco, you need to be prepared to work very hard. You'll have to graduate, of course. And there are exams two weeks from now that you will have to pass to gain acceptance to San Simón. Your teachers will take care of your referrals, but it costs seventy bolivianos just to sit the exam."

I drop my head into my hands. We don't have that kind of money. We need every bit Papá earns to pay for our cell, to pay the council, to pay for protection. If I use our money for this, I'd be risking everything for one test. Taking it and deciding not to go to university after all is not an option. Taking it and failing—impossible.

Profesor Perez walks over to the bookshelf behind his desk and runs a finger along the spines. He pulls out a thin white book and flips through the pages.

"Start with this test prep book. Come back in two days. I'll quiz you, and we'll move on to the next one."

I take the book he hands me.

"This is very ambitious, Francisco."

Yeah. Tell me something I don't know.

After school, we stumble across a pickup game in the park. Pilar and Soledad take one look at my face and start laughing.

"Go," Soledad says as Pilar shoos me toward the dirt field. They lie down in the grass with a blank paper and a half dozen colored pencils between them. I drop my backpack and strip off my white shirt. My pants are going to be filthy after this, but I don't care.

I jog out to the field. My feet stutter to catch the rhythm and shape of the game, and my legs are slow to stretch into a sprint after all this time. But the hours slide by, and my mind is blissfully, perfectly empty.

I haven't felt like this—like myself—in weeks.

After the game is over, we walk to the plaza and spread out below the statue of some Spanish guy who died three hundred years ago. I pull out the test prep book and skim through the pages.

Soledad leans back, her chin pointing straight up to the sky. "Why are you even bothering with that?"

I answer in a low voice, not because I'm afraid Pilar will overhear—she hears everything. More, I guess, because I'm not used to saying these kinds of things out loud. "Papá always pushed so hard for me to do well in school. And lately, I've been thinking maybe this is the only way I can get him out of San Sebastián. We have to go, Pilar and me. But I can't just leave him in there when we do."

Soledad sits up. I can feel her watching me. One side of my face is a normal temperature, and the other is on fire.

"Doesn't your father ever try to get you to leave the prison?" I ask, just to get her eyes off of me.

It works. She leans back again, chin to the sky. "Drugs messed with Papá's head. I don't know if he even knows I'm there most of the time. But if I'm not in the prison, I'm on the street. Girls my age on the streets—sooner or later, they end up selling their bodies so they can eat. I don't have anywhere else to go, not like you. Screw the diploma. Screw university. If I were you, I'd leave tomorrow and never come back."

I keep my eyes on the sky, like the two bashful clouds floating up there are the most fascinating things I've ever seen.

If it comes to that, you could go with us.

I think it, but I'm not brave enough to say it. Not brave enough by half.

November 4

I n the morning, while Papá combs and braids Pilar's hair, I take the test book out onto the balcony and pick up where I left off studying last night. When Pilar is ready, I follow them down the stairs and across the courtyard.

I take Pilar's hand; we wave to Papá and walk beyond the walls. Every time I leave the prison, it's like a weight drops from my shoulders. I don't know how Papá can stand to never be free of that place.

At the end of writing class, Profesora Ortiz asks me to stay behind. I watch everyone clamor to find their friends, to spend the few minutes between classes finding something to laugh about.

"Francisco," she says, "I have read your poems. I see that you are working hard—but I wonder what you're not putting on the paper. I see your father. I see your mother. I see the world around you, but I see nothing of you. Where are *you* in your poems?"

I shrug.

"Francisco?"

"Profesora, I'm not a poet."

"I would beg to differ."

I kick the tile beneath my feet.

"In your next few poems, I want to see emotion, thought, passion—those things that are uniquely yours. Francisco, I want to see your soul."

My arms flap at my sides like a skeleton yanked around on a stand. "I'll try, Profesora. But don't get your hopes up."

After school Thursday, Soledad and I walk to a food cart by Pilar's school where a man is selling escabeche de verduras. We buy three bags, one with extra pepper for Pilar. She loves that spicy shit.

We're a little early, so we lean against the brick wall and suck on the pickled vegetables one at a time, licking the vinegar that runs down our wrists. My lips burn from the peppers steeping at the bottom—the trick is to remember not to touch your eyes for the rest of the day.

"You look tired," I say to Soledad. She does. The skin under her eyes is like a permanent shadow.

She doesn't answer, just flicks her pepper-stained fingers at me.

"I'm serious, Soledad, you look really tired."

"What, you don't have enough on your plate, Francisco? Getting your papá out of prison. Watching over Pilar every waking minute, and some of the unwaking ones, too. Finishing school, and applying to university. Taking your sister to the Altiplano. Really, you're going to start worrying about me, too?"

"Who says I'm just starting?"

Soledad's eyes flare wide. "I don't need you for that."

"Don't call it worry, then." I flick my pepper-stained fingers back at her. "Call it pestering."

She laughs. I stuff the empty plastic bag in my backpack and wipe my fingers on the bricks.

"Seriously, are you not sleeping?"

"When can I rest, Francisco?" Soledad shoves off the wall

and takes a step toward me. "When can I ever let down my guard? Papá is a ghost of the man he was before. Some days I don't even know if he sees me right in front of him. Some nights I barely sleep because he's up and down, and if I don't watch him, he'll unlock the door and then what? Wander somewhere he shouldn't be? Let Red Tito stroll right in?"

"You know you can stay with us."

Soledad's eyebrows raise. "You want me in your bed, Francisco?"

She means it as a joke, but I can't laugh about that. The blood rushes beneath my skin, filling my ears, clouding my eyes like I'm a normal teenager and not some stack of bones rattling through life.

"If it would take the bruises away from your skin, yes. If it meant you could sleep through the night, yes." My voice is thick. I stop talking, and I stuff my hands into my back pockets so if I lose my head I can't reach out and pull her toward me until there is not so much as a gasp of air between us.

She steps closer. I thought there wasn't anything left beneath my ribs, but I feel it now, pumping, banging against my chest. I lean in, so slow, and rest my temple against the side of her head for a second, maybe two. She doesn't flinch away, so I close my eyes and drop my forehead onto her collarbone.

Soledad lays her hands on my chest and tucks the bridge of her nose into the crook of my neck and shoulder. Her breath against that bare triangle of skin burns like chili peppers.

The doors to the primary school bang open, and Soledad

jerks away. The skin of my neck goes cold, and a shiver shakes through me. I blink, and Pilar is between us, holding our hands, jumping up and down, and begging for some escabeche, extra pepper, extra pepper!

Soledad doesn't look at me the rest of the afternoon. But when we settle in a corner of the library, while Pilar reads and I work through the test prep book, Soledad curls on the floor between us and the wall, and she sleeps.

feel it building all that afternoon, all the way home, all evening. It's in the weary tilt of Papá's face, and the way Pilar smooths her doll's frayed hair, and the way my throat constricts when Soledad disappears behind that bolted door for the night.

You want my soul, Profesora Ortiz? Here it is.

The bone that holds my chest together
is cracked down the middle.
Air winds between my organs
dust cakes the crevices
between bone and tissue and blood.
My ribs are pried apart.
This one pulled that way,
that one, this.
And two more beneath,
stretched until they snap,
splayed
in odd directions.

I can't take care of her, and him,
and her, too
and also, somehow, me.

One of us
—maybe all of us—
is going to crack.

And if we're splayed
in odd directions,
if we splinter away from one another
I think it's going to break us all.

November 5

I t's Friday, and just like last week, Soledad makes some excuse after school and takes off in the other direction. I watch her walk away, the narrow V of braids down her back twitching from side to side. I won't see her again until Sunday night maybe, or Monday morning. She rounds the corner two blocks down, and I feel it, like a punch in the gut, when she's gone.

When Pilar walks out of school, she's holding a stick with something hanging off it that looks like a bullet casing, only translucent white, ripped open and trembling with each step she takes.

I lift an eyebrow.

"It's a chrysalis."

"Isn't there supposed to be a butterfly inside?"

"She already left. I don't like the flapping and flying far away part. I like what she left behind."

This kid.

I take her backpack and her empty hand, and we cross town to San Simón. I'm getting to know my way around the place, so it doesn't take long for me to find the admissions office.

Pilar waits on a bench inside while I go up to the counter. A woman in owlish glasses and a wide smile comes to meet me.

"How can I help you, young man?"

I clear my throat. "I would like an application to San Simón for next year."

"Excellent," she replies, and hands me a double-sided form. "You're signed up to take the entrance exams?"

I nod.

"Your scores will be sent directly to us. Fill this out, mail it in, and you will receive notice of your acceptance or denial through the mail as well."

"Thank you." My hands are sweating.

I tuck the form in between the pages of the test prep book in my backpack and sling the straps over my shoulders. Pilar follows me outside. "You're doing this for Papá, aren't you?"

"Yeah."

She nods. "If you can do this, even though I know it's not what you want, I can try to be happy with Abuelo and Abuela, even though it's not what I want."

"Yeah?"

She wraps her arms around my waist and squeezes. I can't fail that test. Not with her, and Papá, and everything riding on it.

When we get back to the cell that night, Pilar hangs the branch from the window so the torn-apart chrysalis dangles there, empty. The sunlight goes right through it. One strong gust of wind, and it'll be gone.

November 6

I used to love weekends. No school. No place I had to be. Rey and I would kick around the days, dreaming mostly of when we would be done with school for good, and our real lives would start. Now the weekends can't go fast enough for me.

In the morning, I help Papá stitch up the holes in his work shirt, and after checking to make sure Red Tito isn't in the courtyard, I bring Pilar down into the sun where she draws on the ground with a discarded pigeon feather.

We spend most of the day in our tiny cell so I can study without distractions. But it's enough to make a person crazy, breathing the same stale air and staring at the same cracked walls all the time.

I know Soledad's gone, but I walk past her cell twice, just in case. I wish I knew for sure that she's okay out there—wherever she is.

I'm never going to get her out of my head just sitting here.

I leave Pilar with Papá and call Reynaldo from the kiosk at the prison, and it takes a little convincing, but we make a plan to meet up in half an hour at the San Simón campus, where there's a grass field with goalposts and actual nets. I lace up my cleats and jog over. If Rey's still mad that I wouldn't get into the shit he's into, he'll get over it on the field. We've always been like that—if anything's off between us, we fix it in the game.

I get there early and wait on the goal line. We've got the whole place to ourselves.

"Hey, man." Reynaldo jogs across the field to meet me. He drops the tough-guy act and slaps me on the shoulders, pulling me into a big hug.

"Hi, Rey," I say, and because I can't trust myself anymore to keep everything under wraps, I slap the ball out of his hands and dribble in the other direction when he pulls away.

We never get the chance to shoot on goal, so today that's all we do. Chip shots and trick shots and hard-driving balls to the corners of the net. We're laughing and digging at each other like we used to, but this isn't like a real game, where the rush and rhythm wipe my mind of all its worries. They hang there, under the laughter, just beneath the layer of sweat dripping off me.

When we give up at last and collapse onto the grass at the back of the net, I tuck the ball under my knees and knot my hands behind my neck.

"Really, Francisco," he says, "how are you doing?"

Looking up through the net, the sky is sectioned off into dozens of soft-sided rectangles. "Honestly?"

"Yeah."

"It's a mess. Every day, Papá is slipping away from us, and from himself. My sister is in this place where she never gets to just be a kid, and where she's never really safe. Me? I can't go off and do what I want with my life and leave them there, like that."

Reynaldo rolls onto his side. "Let me help you. What can I do?"

I shake my head. "Nothing."

"Francisco, what can I do?"

I close my eyes, but the sun still burns through my eyelids, turning the insides red and gold. "There's this test I have to take."

"Don't tell me you need a study partner. You're asking the wrong guy—"

I chuck the ball at Reynaldo, and he swats it away. "The test costs seventy bolivianos, and I don't know how I'm going to scrape together that much money."

"Francisco, seventy bolivianos is nothing."

"Maybe for you."

"I said I wanted to help, didn't I?"

"You'd lend me the money?"

He rolls his eyes. "I'll give you the money. But I'm telling you, if you just come work with me, you won't need whatever test it is that you're so worried about. We'll get our shop open even faster with you selling too . . ."

I hold up a hand, and he closes his mouth over the rest of that sentence.

"I have to do this, Reynaldo." I sit up, so I can say the hard part to his face. "Before I can think about what I want. Before I can even think about our shop, I have to do this."

"Okay," he says, and the joking is over. "I'll send you the money tomorrow."

November 7

The next morning, a priest offers Mass down in the courtyard, reciting the liturgy in a loud voice so even behind closed doors, everyone can hear.

I recite the words on the study sheet in front of me. Branches of government. Systems of democracy. Heads of state. Like a penitent with his tongue outstretched to receive the Eucharist, I've bet everything on this, my salvation. If I can't pass this test, if I can't get Papá out of here, it's not just him who will never be free. It's me, too. It's all of us.

I'm lying on my back and, for once, taking up the whole mattress, my arms and legs sprawled out as far as they can reach. Papá and Pilar are downstairs with some of the other kids drawing with colored chalk on the courtyard stones.

The money for the entrance exams arrived today from Reynaldo. I already spent the whole morning studying, but that doesn't mean I'm done. There's the essay for Profesor Perez, and I still have to write a few more poems. Profesora Ortiz's words echo in my head: *Where are you in your poems?*

I reach back under the corner of the mattress and start digging through the things I have stashed there. In class, we study famous poets, long-dead poets, Spanish poets. What do they know about my life? If I am going to learn how to really write from the raw places, how to make a poem my own, I need Papá as my teacher.

I pull out the stack of poems he wrote for me, unfold the first one he ever gave me years ago, and start reading.

The Naming

It did not occur to me
That in the moment my son
Was placed in my arms—

Small, and warm,
His lips pursed
His eyes wrinkled shut
Not yet ready to look on this harsh world—

It did not occur to me
That I would long for my own father
In that moment.

When I was a child,
My father taught me to go forth in this world

Bearing the past—
our ancestors, our history, our stories—
before me.

Now that I am grown
And holding my son in my arms,
I finally understand
That though he is miles away
I hold my father before me, too.

I wish Abuelo were here now. He wouldn't have a clue about how to get Papá's case through the legal system—he doesn't even speak Spanish. But I think he would know, better than me, how to bring my father back to himself.

The Aymara live with the weight and the wisdom of the past in front of them. I always held what was coming—my future self—up in front of me: what I would be and how I would make a place for myself in the world.

But all that's changing. I never would have guessed prison would be the thing to make me more like my father.

November 8

On Monday morning, Soledad's back again, without a word about where she went, or why. After we drop off Pilar, it's just the two of us. I should have asked where she went when Pilar was still here. Or maybe even made Pilar do the asking and pretended I didn't care either way. But I didn't, so the question hangs there all morning.

It's all I can think about during math and then writing and then science, so I run to catch up with Soledad before history class. I loop my thumbs through the straps on my backpack and shorten my steps to match her smaller ones.

My face is bright red. So what if she knows that I look for her when she's gone? That I miss her when she isn't there?

"Hey," I finally say, "where do you go on the weekends?"

"Out."

I tug the straps on my backpack, and it lifts and then slams back down on my hips. "But where? Where do you sleep?"

"Don't worry about it."

"It's just—are you alone? Is it safe?"

And for the first time ever, she turns her claws on me.

"Who made you my protector, Francisco? Since when do I have to tell you where I am and what I do every minute of every day?"

They rake across my face, and they rip the words from my mouth.

"Oh, so I'm the bad guy now, to care about you." Did I just yell that? The hallways that are always spinning come screeching to a stop.

Everyone is staring at us.

"I'm a giant cojudo because it matters to me whether you end up dead in an alley somewhere? That makes *me* the bad guy?"

I drop my voice to a whisper. "In case you haven't noticed— it's dangerous out there. What's so bad about looking out for each other?"

She just clenches her teeth and glares at me, so I turn and walk away. I never thought I would walk away from her. I feel it crawl under my skin, and slip through my veins. I feel it in every inch of my body. I'm not just a skeleton anymore, and it sucks.

I fling open the door to Profesor Perez's classroom so hard it slams back against the brick, and the noise echoes like a gunshot through the hallway.

look for Soledad when school lets out, but she's already gone. Pilar and I walk to the plaza, and then to the prison, just the two of us. It's Pilar's birthday, so we splurge a little. Dinner is a whole roasted chicken, and we eat every last bit, licking our fingertips and laughing as Papá cracks the bones and sucks out the marrow.

When the chicken is gone, Papá passes around a plate of cocadas and we each take one. I eat mine in nibbles, mincing the pieces of coconut between my teeth.

"How's it going in the wood shop, Papá?" Pilar asks.

"Oh, I'm still learning," he says with a dismissive wave. "They only give me the idiot jobs that can't be messed up: sweeping sawdust, stacking wood, or sanding bedposts."

Pilar takes his hand and lays it against her cheek. "Someday," she says, "you will make the most beautiful furniture. People will come from all over Bolivia to buy your things."

Papá laughs. "Well, I did make one thing on my own, though it's no masterpiece." He stands and leans over the pile of boxes in the corner, reaches behind them, and pulls out a wooden shadow box with nine little shelves inside. He hands it to Pilar, and she runs her fingers over the smooth grain.

"You made this?"

He nods, gesturing to her collection on the wall. "For your things."

Pilar curls into his lap and rests her head against his shoulder. She props the shadow box against her legs. "It's perfect. Thank you, Papá."

The look on her face cuts into me. A shelf and a roasted chicken for her birthday? All I can think of is what a party for a normal kid who doesn't live in prison would be like—balloons, music, cake, and kids everywhere hopped up on sugar.

Not here. Here, all I can think of is what she's not getting.

Papá goes down for roll call. I'm trying to memorize this world map for the entrance exams, and I keep getting Niger and Nigeria and Algeria mixed up. Pilar's trying to help me, and she laughs every time I make the same mistake. I'm tempted to keep screwing it up just so she doesn't stop, but I have to get this right. I have to pass this test.

The intercom quit a while ago, and I know I heard the gate shut and lock. The guard station is closed down for the night. So what's taking Papá so long?

Beneath Pilar's laughter, I hear this yell that lifts the hair on my neck. I jump up and open the door, listening.

"Stay here and lock the door behind me," I whisper.

I run to the balcony. The guards are gone, and the lights are off, but I can still make out a circle of men in the courtyard. They're all yelling and in the middle of it, two big guys are pummeling this smaller figure on the ground.

"*Papá!*"

I run down the stairs and push through the hall, and I hear the sound of their boots in his stomach and their punches landing on his face. "Papá!"

When I get to the circle, it's already breaking up. Red Tito is standing in the corner of the courtyard, watching everything. Men scatter, but my fists are ready, and I'm screaming, screaming at the cowards who did this to face me.

I feel a hand on my ankle, and I drop down to the ground. "Papá."

He rolls over, slowly, onto his stomach and spits blood onto the ground.

"Papá." My voice breaks.

He grabs my hand, and I gently lift him up. I drape his arm over my shoulder, and we stand together. I don't know where to hold on—if they got his kidneys or his ribs. I'm afraid to even wrap my arm around him to help him to the stairs.

"How did this happen, Papá? I don't understand—you paid up, right? We should be protected."

He coughs, and more blood spills from his lips. His voice is raspy. "Some of the men in here are outside the council's control."

My mind is racing. "Why you? Why, all of a sudden, are those guys after you?"

His steps are so slow. He weighs almost nothing. "It doesn't matter."

"It matters, Papá!" If he wasn't so badly hurt, I would take him by the shoulders and shake him.

My father looks up into my face. "They wanted you to bring drugs into the prison for them. Just once, they said. The guards would never know, they said."

His words are like ice on my skin. "They did this to you because of me?" And the other fight he got into—was that because of me too?

"No, my son." He pauses to catch his breath. "They did this because they are desperate. They did this because they are cruel men. Don't worry about me. It's over. They've exacted their price for my refusal."

"You don't know that. You don't know they won't try again."

"Well, they can't have my son." He puts one foot in front of the other and groans as we carefully climb the stairs. "What are they going to do to me? Take my freedom? Too late. Take my dignity? Too late. Take my life?" His head ticks to the side. "That may be a blessing for you and your sister in the end."

We stop in front of our cell door. "Don't say that, Papá. Don't even think it."

"Too late," he whispers.

November 9

S oledad doesn't wait for us in the morning. I thought it was just a little fight between us. I didn't think she would cut me out for good. I take Pilar's hand as we leave the prison and pull her to a side street.

Pilar held it together last night when I brought Papá into the cell. And she tried to smile when he saw us off to school this morning. But now that he's not here to see, tears drip down her face like melted wax.

I see Soledad in class, but it's like before, when I was a stranger to her. I watch her when she isn't looking. I wish I could tell what she's thinking. But she doesn't even look at me. Not once.

Pilar and I go to the plaza after school. I try to focus on the paper in front of me; the entrance exams are only five days away. The wind is halfheartedly tossing around the tops of the palm trees over our heads. The serrated shadows cover the list of vocabulary words in front of me and pull away again. Shadows, then light, and then shadows again.

Pilar sits up suddenly and peers across the plaza, shading the sun from her eyes. I follow where she's looking.

"It's not her."

I tell Pilar this has nothing to do with her, that Soledad loves her like a sister, and it's me who ruined everything. But one thing about all this time in prison—I know my sister now. When she chews on the side of her lip like that, she's thinking about Mamá.

And it's happened all over again for her—without a word, without any explanation, she's been tossed aside.

Pilar slumps back against the bench and drops her chin to her chest. She shreds a leaf between her fingers, pulling the veins out one by one.

"Hey, don't you want to keep that? It would look nice on the shelf by the others."

Pilar shakes her head. Her chin doesn't lift from her chest. "What's the point?"

She's not supposed to give up. Not Pilar. I flip over the vocab list in time to catch the words as they untangle themselves in my mind. I usually turn away so no one will see me write, but I don't know what my sister and I have to hide from each other anymore.

> *I think those eyes see more*
> *than they let on.*
> *She's just a kid*
> *a nine-year-old girl.*

What scares me
is she sees it all.
Her mind is swimming with things
finned and full of teeth
slithering, slinking from dark hole
to darker hole.

Those things,
they worm their way inside a person
and I'm not sure
you can ever coax them out again.

It feels better, to get it down. My mind is quieter, like when I'm on the fútbol field and the game wipes my head clean. Maybe it's not such a bad thing, becoming more like Papá, if putting words to the page can do that for me now, too.

Later that night, I'm studying, Pilar is scraping the floor with a rock, and Papá is lying on the mattress, staring at the wall.

Suddenly there's this crash outside, and then a loud, long wail. We throw open our cell door and crowd onto the balcony. Down in the courtyard, a boy a little younger than Pilar is lying on the ground, screaming. His mother bends over him, her hands fluttering above the boy's blistering skin. A crowd packs around him like ice on a wound.

As the boy is lifted by a dozen hands and carried to the gate, still screaming, murmurs pass along the balcony.

"The whole thing crashed down on him."

"He was just playing."

"He shouldn't have been running near a pot of boiling water."

"Where else are the kids supposed to play?"

There's shouting and arguments at the guard station as the prisoners push against the gate and the guards push back. Finally, the kid is passed through and the mother follows, sobbing into her hands. The father is left on this side of the gate, gripping the bars and calling after his son.

Papá pulls Pilar and me back into our cell and locks the door. But he can't shut out the sounds of the grieving father down in the courtyard, shouting until there's nothing of his voice left to carry the pain.

November 10

The prison is quiet in the morning. Even the guards seem somber as they open the gate and usher the pack of kids out. That could have been any of us last night. It could have been me. It could have been Pilar.

My sister holds my hand even tighter than normal. We stay with the group all the way to school. I wish Soledad was here with us, not just for me—because everything seems a little better when she's close—but for Pilar, because she needs her, too.

The worst thing is seeing Soledad at school—the flick of her braids as she turns the corner. Or the way the air changes when she's near me. I can feel her there, but I can't even look at her.

In writing class, she sits two chairs back and to the left. In algebra, she's directly behind me. In history, I'm all the way at the front, and she's all the way at the back. But the distance doesn't make it better. It's worse, somehow.

I thought maybe after a few days, she'd quit being mad. I thought she'd come back to us. I thought after all we've been through, I meant something to her.

I stay late after school, and Profesor Perez quizzes me on the study guide I took home. I get only thirty minutes to work with him each day before I have to sprint to pick up Pilar.

For thirty minutes straight, I try to block it all out—the little boy from last night, and Soledad, and Papá. I try to focus.

If I don't pass this test, I don't know how I'll be able to live with myself. I need this to work for Papá, and for me and Pilar, too.

I exchange the old test prep book for a new one and zip my backpack closed, ready to run to make it to Pilar's school in time. Well, not in time. I'm late enough that her teachers watch me come and go with withering looks, but not so late that she's just left outside all alone.

Maybe it's better, all this rushing from place to place. All this stress, all this studying. It's something to do besides miss her.

November 11

've been getting up early to study in the mornings, and the lack of sleep makes my eyes burn, but I'm getting better at this stuff, I can tell.

When I've had enough, I chuck the study guide onto the floor and roll over. Pilar is sitting at the bottom of the blankets, her slight shoulders hunched over. I crawl to the edge of the mattress and stretch the soreness out of my neck.

Papá is still sleeping. He hasn't been back to the wood shop since he was jumped the other night, so I've been helping Pilar get ready for school and cooking all our meals, and Pilar is the one now trying to bring Papá back to us.

She stretches out her palm toward me, and there's this brown thing cupped inside.

"What's that?" I ask my sister through a yawn.

"It's for you."

I pluck it out of her hands. "Thanks, Pilar. It's really nice."

"No—look at it."

Okay. It's a brown lump, like maybe a shell or a nut or something, only it's split in half. I turn it over and it rocks a little in my palm. The inside is nothing like the outside. It's not rough or bumpy or coarse. It's smooth as sandstone, all soft curves and hollow spaces.

"Look at it, Francisco."

I *am*. What does she want from me?

Pilar traces her finger around the outline of the smooth inner space. "See?" she says. "It's a heart."

I squint to see what she sees. I don't get it. And then, suddenly, I do. I was looking at it all wrong. The empty space where the seeds used to be splits into two symmetrical curves at the top that narrow to a point below.

"You'd never know it was in there," Pilar says, "if you only ever saw the outside."

I tuck the shell inside my pocket, drape an arm over my sister's shoulder, and plant a kiss in her hair. Prison has taken so much from her, from me, from all of us, but it's given me this, too.

November 12

I don't know who writes these study manuals—nobody who wants kids to actually like learning. Nobody who wants kids to think the decision to go to university is a good one.

But I'm like a fox who has decided the only way out of the steel jaws holding him down is to chew off his own leg. No matter how much I hate it, I don't stop. I study like there is no other thing I could possibly be doing. I study like my life depends on it.

Because even if it doesn't, I think Papá's might.

So it's a Friday night, and I'm making outlines, underlining words and looking them up, and filling in a thousand note-cards. Papá watches me. He doesn't ask what all this sudden studying is about, and I don't explain. I can't imagine anything worse than telling him my plan and then not being accepted into San Simón.

Papá and me, we're the same now. We're both trapped. Doing what we have to just to make it through the day. To not joggle loose the memory of what it felt like to walk in a world that rolled over to share the soft curves and hollow spaces with us.

November 13

I don't dream anymore about Mamá, or fútbol. Or even Soledad. But still, I miss her.

I can't talk to Papá, not about this. I open my notebook and turn to a fresh page.

In seventh grade,
we took a trip to the salt flats:
a mirror laid over the high plains
reflecting the sky
reflecting the ground
reflecting the sky.

Droves of pink birds swarmed
the alpine lakes.
In the middle of all that nothing—
flamingoes.
Thousands of them.

They mate for life, you know.
They fly, always, in the same flock.
They nest, always, by the same lake.
But what happens if one day,
one of them veers away?

What happens to the one left behind?

Does he still build a nest every summer
for eggs that will never be laid?

Does he still call out for her
all those years later?

t's the day before the exam and I've been studying all day. I
don't think anything is even sinking in anymore. I think best
when I'm moving.

I jump up. "I'm going out."

The pickup game is in a dirt field on the other side of town
from where I used to play, so I don't know anyone, and no one
knows me. The goals are fence posts, with a rope for a crossbar.
In the game, I can push and cuss and tackle, and nobody calls
me out for it. We're all fighting out there, battling something
besides one another.

Shirts and skins. Pretty soon, my team is losing, so I throw
a couple extra elbows. They slide off of sweat-soaked ribs while
my mark yanks me back with a sharp tug on my shirt. *¡Pucha!* I
should have picked skins.

I take a hard tackle and roll in the dust. My mark has me
beat, and it's just him and the goal now. He rips one past our
keeper and opens his arms to the sky like the Cristo rising over
the city. Just for a second, though. There's no net, so he quickly
drops the act and jogs off to fetch the ball. It's the rule. You
shoot it, you chase it.

The rest of us go for water. I'm still spitting out the grit
of the field when a hand clamps down on my shoulder.

"Picked the wrong team again, eh, Francisco?"

I whirl around. "Reynaldo!" It's good to see him. I take
a step to close the space between us, but something stops me.
"Your má let you come back home yet?"

"Ha!—I wouldn't go back if she did. I'm living like a king."

Reynaldo circles behind me and comes up on the other side. I lean against the bench and stretch my hamstrings. I'm out of practice, and every single one of my muscles is letting me know it.

"Profesor Perez asked about you again last week."

"You think I care about school?"

Yeah, well, he never did. Neither did I, before.

"You know, Francisco, this is crazy good money. I've got my own place now—I don't even have to share with anybody. You could stay with me. Bring Pilar if you have to."

I reach out to steady myself on the bench. A bed, off the floor. Food to eat, whenever we're hungry. A life here, in the city, where we could visit Papá every day. A normal life. The roof of my mouth is tacky. I can't seem to swallow.

I've been killing myself trying to find a way through all this, and the answer just falls into my lap. So easy. But all the questions have changed.

I straighten, stretching my arm over my head and rolling out my ankles. "And we'll be doing what, Reynaldo? Selling drugs?" I try to make my tone light, but I hear an edge creep into it. I just wanted some time to myself. I just needed a minute.

"Yeah. What else?"

I drop my arms and look my friend full in the face. "If being in prison doesn't kill my father, then me selling drugs, and ending up there too—only actually deserving it—that would do it for sure."

"We won't get caught, Francisco. Don't be such a cobarde."

The tension that has been fizzing inside me all day goes flat. This isn't the fight I want. "Look, thanks for the offer. I mean it. I just can't."

"You can't." He throws his hands up in the air. "And what about our shop? I was doing this for us, you know."

It's over, and I know it. Whoever I was before, whatever mattered to me before—I can't be that guy anymore. Everything I'm trying to hold together—it's too much. It's bigger than just me.

I shake my head. "I can't open the shop with you, Rey. Not now."

"So what—you're too good for me now?" He closes the distance between us. "You'd rather live in prison? You'd rather be poor as shit than be like me? Is that it?"

Reynaldo plants both hands on my chest and shoves. He follows, step for step, as I stumble backward. He shoves again. His lip is curled up and sticking to his gums, and I don't see even one hint of my friend in that face. I don't know this guy. And I don't want to.

He comes at me again, and this time, he doesn't shove, he punches. Three quick fists in the ribs. The breath coughs out of me, and my arms close over my stomach. For the first time, ever, I don't hit back. Instead, I sidle out of reach. "I'll see you around." And I walk away.

Under his breath, in a voice my friend Reynaldo never had, he says, "You better hope you don't."

November 14

The college entrance exams are held on the Sunday before the last week of school.

I leave my backpack by the cell door and tell Papá I'm heading out for a bit.

He just nods, but Pilar stands and squeezes my waist in a quick hug.

"You can do it," she whispers.

I step out onto the balcony and close the door behind me. Soledad's gone—not that she would be talking to me if she weren't. Still, my steps slow as I pass her door, listening for any sound of her inside.

Nothing.

I walk to school, where the other kids waiting to take the test mill around the locked front doors, jumpy but trying not to show it. So it's not just me, then.

We walk as a jittery herd to the university and sit in tidy rows while the proctor takes roll. This is it. Everything depends on this.

After every rule the proctor reads from the test book, he

glares at us over the rim of his bifocals. We fill in our names. My pencil keeps slipping out of my fingers like I never learned how to write.

We wait.

A muscle in my neck twitches. I roll my head from side to side, and every joint in my spine pops.

"You may begin."

We flip over our booklets. The clock on the wall counts down the seconds, each tick echoing against the glass. The hours are a blur. Sweaty hands, too many questions, too many other hunched backs over scribbling pencils.

I'm almost finished when the proctor says, "Put down your pencils and close your examination books." He moves through the aisles, collecting them one by one.

It's the hardest test I've ever taken. But then, I've never cared how I did on a test before. Maybe it's the caring that makes it so hard.

I'm tired. My eyes are bleary.

I run all the way back to the prison. If I show up sweaty from running back, maybe Papá will think I was just out playing fútbol with the guys, and leave it at that.

Before I go up to the cell, I make a call at the kiosk. I punch in the numbers and wait while the phone rings and rings and then clicks over to voice mail.

"Reynaldo, it's me. Francisco."

I hate leaving messages. I never know what to say.

"Listen, I know you're mad at me, but it's not what you think. I just can't do anything that would hurt Pilar or Papá right now. They've been through enough, you know?"

I pause. What—am I expecting him to answer?

"Look, that test I had to take—it's because I'm trying to get into university next year. It's going to be really tough to go to school and pay rent on my own. How about this—I get out of the prison and you get out of . . . whatever you've gotten into. And we get a place together. We won't be able to live like kings. But it could be good. Think about it, okay?"

do the laundry so Papá can sleep. I play futbolito with José and the guys in the courtyard for an hour or so. When we're done, we sit in a clump on the pavement. Our sweat dries on our skin as the guys laugh and jeer and trade jokes at one another's expense. It's almost like before, in my old neighborhood, hanging with my ex-friends.

I walk to the cancha to pick up some groceries. Everywhere I go, I'm on edge, flinching every time I think I see Soledad out of the corner of my eye.

By the time I get back to our cell, it's like sparks from a burned-out light socket in my fingertips. I grab my notebook and a pen and lean into the wall so Pilar and Papá can't see what I'm writing.

> *If you try to touch a wildcat,*
> *run your fingers along*
> *the strong line of her jaw*
> *she'll take your hand in her teeth;*
> *you'll never see it again.*

> *If you try to keep pace with a wildcat*
> *she'll stretch her legs*
> *and with a flick of her tail*
> *devour the earth in bounds*
> *and agile leaps;*
> *you'll never see her again.*

But if you stand tall
and still
don't seek her eyes
don't ask
what she can't give,
if you stay still as a tree
driving roots down
into the ground
where only rock and castaway dust
can be found,
she just might twine around your legs
climb into your arms
drape herself there,
and your limbs will grow strong enough
to hold her up.

November 15

"**H**ey, Francisco—wait up."

My feet stutter to a stop, and the rush of students moves through the hallway around me like leaves blowing around a trash can. But I don't turn. It actually hurts, to hear her say my name.

Soledad comes alongside me, and she stops, too. Two trash cans. The leaves spin in little cyclones. The crowd is jeering, snickering.

But I hardly hear them because just then, her hand closes over my wrist and my whole arm goes numb. She looks at me, full in the face, and I couldn't move now even if I wanted to.

"Has your Papá taught you what an *ayllu* is?"

What? Nothing from her all week, and this is what she wants to tell me? "Maybe? I don't know. He probably did and I wasn't listening. Why?"

Soledad starts walking, and she pulls me along with her. "It's how everybody is taken care of without needing money. If you live by the lake, you give others in your *ayllu* some of your fish. If you live in the jungle, you share your fruit. If you live on the Altiplano, you share your wool, and everybody helps everybody else till and sow and harvest the crops. It's the only way our people have survived all these centuries in such a harsh climate."

"Okay. What does that that have to do with—"

But she just keeps going. "There's no *ayllu* in the prison. That place runs on despair and bribes and fear." She pulls me into a corner away from the rush of students, and we lean against the bricks, facing each other. She doesn't take her hand away.

"Every weekend I go to the hills to make an offering to Pachamama."

"Soledad—"

She waves my question away. "You think it's ridiculous. I knew you would. That's why I didn't tell you where I was going. I didn't want you to think *I* was ridiculous."

Okay. I'm listening.

"I thought if the spirits knew how much I wanted a life out of the prison, how much I wanted an *ayllu* to belong to, they would help me find it."

The hall is emptying, the students funneling into classrooms, and the sound of the doors closing behind them one by one echoes through the halls. It goes quiet. Everybody's cramming for the end-of-year exams.

When Soledad begins to speak again, her voice is so soft I have to duck my head to hear her. "What I didn't realize is that you and me and Pilar were becoming our own little *ayllu*."

Soledad takes a step toward Profesor Perez's classroom,

and her hand falls away from my arm. She pauses by the window.

"When I realized that, it scared me. Not because you don't have the right to care about me. I'm glad you worry. I'm glad you're here for me. And"—she looks at the ground and the sunlight drags shadows from her eyelashes down her cheeks—"it has meant everything to have you and Pilar—to have somebody to take care of, too. I finally found what I've wanted all along, just in time to lose it."

I reach out a hand—I don't know, to cup the curve of her elbow or to trace the line of her jaw—but I stop myself and let it fall back to my side again.

"See, if I need you, then what happens to me when you're gone?"

She doesn't give me a chance to answer. She opens the door to Profesor Perez's class and slips through. And even if she had given me the space for my words, what could I have said—that I'm not going anywhere? That I'd never leave her?

I can't make those kinds of promises right now.

We walk together to get Pilar. Soledad doesn't say any more—she doesn't have to. Just having her here with me again is like an electric current under my skin.

When Pilar sees us, she runs over with a squeal and throws her arms around Soledad's neck. As we walk together toward the plaza, Pilar links her arm through Soledad's so one hand is free, her fingers curled around some small thing in her palm.

"What's that?" Soledad asks.

"A snail shell." Pilar opens her hand so we can see the brown whorls. "The snail is long gone. Maybe eaten by a bird or something. Maybe it grew its own wings so it didn't need a house on the ground anymore."

"It's really pretty, Pilar," Soledad says, meeting my eyes over my sister's head. "You find treasure everywhere you go, don't you?"

Pilar smiles and tucks the snail shell into her shirt pocket. She swings the hand of the wild girl beside her back and forth and back and forth.

Maybe I can't shield Pilar from this life we've been dragged into. But maybe I don't have to—at least not alone. I'm still not sure how Soledad came to be part of *us*, or even what changed and brought her back again, but however it came to be, we need her.

I need her.

stir the rice while Pilar lies on the mattress, kicking her heels in the air and combing her doll's hair.

Papá is sitting up. The bruises on his face are yellowing, and he only grunts in pain a little when he moves now.

"So," he says. "The last day of school is in a couple of days."

Pilar rolls over, her arms stretched out to Papá, pleading. "Mariela asked if I can come over next week. She has a new puppy. Please, Papá, can I go?"

Papá's lips twitch at the corners. "I tell you what. You do your very best on your exams, and you can go see your friend as often as your brother will take you in the weeks before you leave for your grandparents' home."

It's my turn, now, to get the full force of my sister's pleading. "Please, Francisco? Please?"

"We'll go on Monday. Get her address tomorrow at school, okay?"

There's more to say, like how when summer break starts, we'll be here every morning and every night with Papá when he's not in the wood shop. Like how once there's no more studying to do, when there's nothing to do but wait, I'll do all the laundry and all the cooking during the day so we can spend as much time as possible with him.

Like how I'm going to find some way to get a job during the day so before we leave I can pay the rent for a few months and get Papá a bed off the floor and a little table and chair so he doesn't have to eat on the ground like an animal.

But all that can wait. Right now, Soledad has come back to us. Pilar's happy, and Papá is almost smiling. Everything else can wait.

A *bang* wakes me in the middle of the night, and I shoot straight up, my pulse racing. That was just my dream, right? But my ears are ringing. My skin is alive, lightning dancing from one hair to the next.

Not just a dream, then. What was it?

A crash?

A gunshot?

A scream?

November 16

Soledad said she would wait for us in the morning. But when Pilar and I go past her father's cell on the way out of the prison, the lock is missing from the door, and Soledad's gone. Her father is gone. And I feel it then, high in the back of my throat. Panic.

"Where is she?" Pilar asks. "I thought— Why would she leave without telling us?"

"I don't know."

She isn't at school either. I run through the halls, duck into every room and stairwell and broom closet even though I know I'm going to be late and the director is yelling at me to get to class. I finally do, moving from room to room through the long morning like I'm supposed to.

"Francisco, are you okay?" Profesor Perez asks, calling me back from the rush of students pouring into the hallway.

"Have you seen Soledad?"

"No." He seems confused by the question.

I try to go, but he grips my shoulder. "Francisco, you'll

be here tomorrow, to turn in your work and sit your end-of-year exams?"

"I'll be here." I shake off his hand and run.

When I finally get out of there and pick up Pilar, she cinches her sweater around her waist and runs with me. Both our backpacks bang against my shoulders, out of time with my thumping feet. We search the cancha, the biblioteca, the plaza, but we don't find Soledad anywhere. I can't think. It's hiccups in my breath. It's pinpricks in my eyes.

"We'll find her, Francisco." Pilar says. Her hand is sweaty and gripping mine. I don't know who is taking care of whom anymore.

We search for hours. The last place I think to look is the last place I ever would have wanted to find her. At the end of the alley under the stone arch leading to Reynaldo's broken city, I finally see her. My heart stops. She's huddled in a corner. She looks so small.

I drop Pilar's hand and sprint over.

The right side of her face is purple. One eye is swollen shut, and blood is smeared above her ear. I think I see a tremor ripple through her. And then I break all the rules. I lift her up and hold her head against me as gently as I can. I wish I could cover every inch of her.

Over her head, I watch Reynaldo approach, his hands raised, his movements deliberate. "Francisco, I swear, she came to us like that."

"This happened to you in the prison?" I whisper. "Or on the street? Who did this to you?"

She groans in response.

Reynaldo moves closer. Who is it this time I'm looking at? My friend? Or that other guy?

I tilt Soledad's face up so I can see her eyes. The pupils are dilated; her eyes are glassy, barely blinking.

"Come back with us," I whisper. "Don't stay here tonight. You know this isn't a good place."

She doesn't answer. Her eyes don't focus on me, or anything.

"Come back with us. You can sleep between Pilar and me tonight. We'll keep you safe."

"No." It's barely more than a whisper.

"I can't leave you here, but I have to get Pilar back. Soledad, please."

"I'll never go back there."

My eyes find Reynaldo.

I hear the tremble in my voice. "One night. Can you keep her safe for one—"

"Francisco," he says, and there they are, the eyes of my friend—not the dealer, not the tough. "No one will touch her."

My face is hot, but my fingers are like icicles hanging from my arms. Pilar and I have to go *now*. We have to hurry if we're going to make it back to Papá before the gate closes.

"Can you trust me, Francisco?"

Trust?

I trust my father to find a way through his grief. I trust

Pilar to bend and shift without breaking. I'm not sure if I trust Reynaldo anymore, but I don't have a choice.

Pilar and I weren't supposed to leave Cochabamba for a few more weeks. We were going to wait until the very last day before my eighteenth birthday. But that's all changed now. It's time to obey my father's wishes. Every last one of them.

"Tomorrow," I whisper into Soledad's hair. "I have to take my exams in the morning. And then I'll come get you, and we'll leave together, the three of us." She closes her eyes, but she doesn't push me away. The fingers of one hand curl into the collar at my neck and pull my skin closer to her skin.

That's answer enough for me.

Pilar and I run back to the prison. The light is changing, and I know we're cutting it close—too close. We cross back under the prison walls and slip through the gate just as the guard is closing it. Every light in San Sebastián is on, and the guards are inside, dashing around, turning out every cell and speaking in sharp bursts over their radios.

Something is wrong.

Papá's face is an ashy gray. Behind him, the prison is in uproar; my father's still form is framed by a halo of chaos. The news is on everyone's lips: Red Tito is dead. His body was found early that morning, gouges like claw marks carved into his chest, a pair of puncture wounds like bite marks in his neck.

All night, the men stand in rows in the courtyard while the guards count and re-count and pull one prisoner after another into a back room for interrogations. Floodlights illuminate the whole place, and the moths swarm to them, fracturing the light as it falls.

I know Papá hasn't eaten, so I make dinner and carry a plate down to him. The potatoes are okay, but the rice is somehow crunchy and soggy at the same time. It's the best I can do.

I stuff our backpacks full of everything I can think of: Pilar's doll, her Sunday clothes, the map Papá made for our bus trip to the Altiplano. I run my fingers along the lining of my coat to check that the money for the bus ticket is still stitched in place.

I leave Pilar's collection of discarded things on the shelf for Papá so the place won't look so empty once we're gone. I can't think about what it's going to be like here for him after we leave.

Hours pass, and finally the guards go back outside and the prisoners shuffle to their cells. My father's face is overlapping shadows. He doesn't even try to smile, just locks the door, then lies down on the mattress and rolls over to face the wall.

I fill in the last row of boxes on the application to San Simón with the return address from my grandparents' letter.

It's done. I only hope it's enough.

November 17

I n the morning, I help Pilar lift her backpack onto her shoulders; it's way heavier than normal. Papá walks down the stairs with us and across the courtyard, but the guards are here, on this side of the gate, and they won't let us pass.

"The prison is on lockdown—nobody goes in or out today."

Papá nods, like he expected this. "My children just need to go to school. It's their last day. They have end-of-year exams to take."

"No. Nobody leaves today."

I can feel my pulse begin to pick up. Pilar sidles behind me.

Papá cocks his head to the side. "I know you'd rather the children weren't here at all. It would be easier for you if you didn't have to answer for their safety. Especially now, with such violence inside these walls."

The guard taps a finger against his rifle. "You're wasting your time. This is a homicide investigation."

"If my son passes his exams today, he will graduate with a secondary school diploma. No one from my family has ever held a secondary school diploma. No one from my family has ever been given that kind of opportunity."

The guard doesn't care—that much is clear. My breath comes in rasps. I have to get to Soledad. I have to get to school.

Papá lowers himself onto one knee, and then the other. "I may never leave this place. But please, let my children have the chance for a different life than this one." He lifts his hands in supplication. "Please."

The guard shuffles his weight from foot to foot. He looks over his shoulder at the gate behind him. "I can't."

Papá reaches into his shirt pocket and pulls out a roll of bills. It's everything we have.

"Papá, no!"

The guard doesn't say anything, but he takes the money, reaches behind him, and opens the gate a sliver, just wide enough for Pilar and me to slip through.

I have to go. Now. It's what Papá wants, only I can't seem to move. Pilar closes the space between them and wraps her arms around Papá's neck.

He and I have never been able to say what we need to, face-to-face. Maybe I could now, if my throat would open. But it doesn't, and I still can't. So I kneel beside them, and the three of us hold on as tight as we possibly can.

Two breaths, and Papá pushes us gently away, to the other side of the world. "Go now—quickly. And don't come back."

Pilar and I pass hand in hand through the gate. I look

back and Papá is still on his knees, framed in the doorway, waving good-bye.

I didn't cry when Papá was put in prison, or when Mamá left us, or even when we had to move in to San Sebastián. But if Papá has lost us and he's lost hope then I think maybe everything is lost.

My eyes itch. The back of my throat burns. I pull Pilar with me in the space between the brick wall and the row of parked cars, and the water spills from my eyes and my nose like marrow seeping out of a cracked bone.

force myself to concentrate on my end-of-year exams. I turn in all my poems to Profesora Ortiz (even the embarrassing ones), and hand in the essay to Profesor Perez.

I should say good-bye, or at least thanks, to my teachers, but every second I have to wait until Soledad is beside me, before I can be sure she's all right, makes panic rise up like it's going to choke me from the inside.

When the day is finally over, I dodge kids ripping papers out of their notebooks and throwing them into the air, and guys kicking their backpacks down the hallway like they're shooting on goal. I squeeze through a crowd dancing and singing, flinging their arms all over the place, past a group of girls laughing and hugging each other, and I'm out—through the double doors of the school for the last time.

As soon as I'm free, I run the whole way, to grab some food at a street-side market, to drop my application in the mail, to buy tickets at the bus station, and finally, to pick up my sister at the primary school.

Pilar is ready when I get to her. Her jaw is tight, and her eyes are wide. This is never what she wanted, to leave Papá. It's never what either of us wanted. I take her hand, and together we run for it.

When we pass under the arch to Reynaldo's broken city, I don't see Soledad anywhere.

"Soledad!" Pilar shouts while I dash through the place, tossing blankets in the air and ripping tarps off the shacks. "Soledad!"

The kids are wide-eyed, flinching away from me like I'm some kind of monster.

I wince at the fear on their faces. I'm not a monster—maybe I was, before. Maybe that's where I was headed. But I'm not. Not anymore. I unclench my fists.

If she's gone, though, if something has happened to her—

"Hey—Francisco."

I whirl around. It's Reynaldo. His hands are up, and his face is pleading.

"Hey, man, it's okay," he says.

"Where is she?"

He lowers his hands and beckons. "She's resting. She's waiting for you."

I'm shaking, and it's Pilar who follows Reynaldo, pulling me after her. We go through another arch and up a winding staircase into a room with carpet on the floor and lamps in the corners and a sofa against the wall, where Soledad is sleeping, a blanket pulled up under her chin.

Pilar runs over to her, whispers in her ear, and smooths the hair away from her bruises. Soledad sits up slowly, watching Reynaldo and me through her one good eye.

Time slows, my breath slows, and it's like even the dust and dander sifting through the air all around us slows. Soledad stands and moves to my side. This girl who doesn't trust anyone trusts me. Pilar kisses Soledad's hand and clasps it between both of hers.

Reynaldo watches as the three of us leave together. He

lifts a hand to wave from the top of the stairs, and now that the weight has fallen from my chest, now that my hands are filled with Pilar's on one side, and Soledad's on the other, I can smile in return.

A real smile. A full one.

At the bus station, I hand Soledad and Pilar their tickets. We climb on board and even in the tight spaces and the noise and the still air, my breaths come easily. We're here. We made it.

Soledad and Pilar take one seat, and I sit across the aisle from them, close enough to help my sister shift her heavy backpack, and close enough to reach out and brush the back of Soledad's hand. If I knew how, I would draw that sadness from her cheeks, and her eyes, and her mouth.

Instead, I keep my hands clasped in my own lap. Soledad sleeps, and I watch the flutter of her eyes under closed lids, the flicker of a pulse at her neck. A slant of sunshine filters across her forehead, her torso, and the backs of her hands.

There is blood under her fingernails.

The day fades, and the bus rumbles over the broken highway. The road climbs steadily up into the hills. To reach the Altiplano, you have to go up, over the high mountain passes. The road, sometimes paved, sometimes not, hugs the side of peaks. If you look over the edge, you can see bits of gravel tumbling down to a graveyard of cars with blown-out windows, rusted doors, and broken frames lining the bottom of the ravine.

When we reach the top, the earth levels out again, rolling and barren, and stretching as far as you can see. We pass a man working a small rectangle of tilled earth. We pass a military checkpoint, and we all get out, our bags held in front of us while men with machine guns walk a drug-sniffing dog down the line. We pass empty stretches of land where only wandering llamas and vicuñas live. The orange and pink light from the fading sun drips over terraced hillsides and jumbled rock piles that mark abandoned mines.

Pilar whimpers and shifts in her sleep. Soledad tucks herself against my sister's sleeping form. But before she sleeps again, she finds my eyes, reaches a hand across the narrow aisle and rests it for a moment against my cheek, her fingers curling behind my jaw.

I can't help myself, I lean into her hand and press my lips against her palm. Soledad's eyes flare and fade. Her hand falls, and then her eyelids, too.

In the city, wrinkles of mountains surrounded us at all times like cracks around the rim of an eggshell sky. But it's different here on the Altiplano. It's not really the air, or the quiet, or even the Andes in the distance. It's the sky. It doesn't keep to its borders. It's all-encompassing. It's everything.

The earth stretches as far as I can see, to where the beginnings of blue shiver on the horizon, where the air is so thin my lungs shrink in on themselves just to feel full, where the only scar in the ground leads to abandoned mineshafts deep in the earth, and the sky is too much to take in with a single glance.

I take Pilar's hand as we step off the bus. There is no luggage to hand down from the roof. We have nothing but our backpacks. But we're together.

I tug Papá's hand-drawn map out of my pocket and turn it as the bus chortles along the road, coughing dust and exhaust over us like incense spilling out of a priest's thurible, blessing the last leg of our journey.

When Pilar was born, we came here once to show the new baby to our grandparents. All I remember from that trip is a curving, dusty road ending in a cluster of squat buildings nestled against the hills. I wait for Soledad to come in line with Pilar and me; she catches my hand, and the three of us start down that same dirt road together.

We should have taken the night bus so we had all day to walk. But I didn't think that far ahead. So when night comes, we lie side by side on the edge of the road. Before, I might have been scared. Now, after all we've been through just to get here, the gato montés and the foxes will damn well leave us alone.

Pilar invents her own constellations and whispers their stories in Soledad's ear, tracing the figures in the air. The sky is smothered with stars, with no city lights to mute them. The mountain peaks in the distance are little more than jagged shadows. I shift my backpack beneath my head like a pillow and look up. I swear if the mountains weren't there, the sky would wrap underneath me too, like a big bubble of stars.

It's quiet, not like in the city, where restless cats yowl at the darkness and taxis weave through the streets at all hours. If there is even anything alive out here besides those lonely vicuñas, it isn't saying a thing. My head falls to the side, away from the stars. Soledad is watching me over Pilar's head. Her eyes are black pools. The starlight shines in her hair.

It's a good thing Pilar is there, asleep, between the two of us.

Still, I reach across and run my hand up and down her arm, chafing the goose bumps from her skin. I blow on my palm to warm it and lay it against her bare neck. "You're cold," I whisper.

She shakes her head. "Do you know that every night I spent in San Sebastián, I wrote a wish on a scrap of paper and dropped it over the prison wall? Every night. Do you know what my wish was, Francisco?"

"What?" My voice cracks on the cold air.

"This. Freedom. I'd rather spend every night of my life shivering in the dirt than in that prison or on the street under some tough's *protection*."

I can't hold those eyes.

"Francisco, look at me."

My eyes flick back up to hers.

"*Ven.*"

And I do.

I lean up and over Pilar, and Soledad pulls me up and over to the other side of her. I take her face in my hands and kiss her. Those black eyes flutter closed as she moves against me.

Her lips are salt and wind and fire on mine. She presses the length of her along the length of me, and the stars start spinning above. The shadow mountains disappear, and the bubble of stars is spinning, spinning, spinning all around us.

November 18

I t's not a short walk, but it's an easy path to follow. There's just the one road. By midmorning, I can see the low buildings like a smudge against the hillside, and by the time the sun is above our heads, we're there.

The whole community comes out to welcome us: two dozen people, not one of them younger than my father. They offer us coca like Papá said they would, and I mumble my way through Aymara words I half remember.

My abuela kisses our cheeks and takes our hands. She's round and short, but her grip is so much stronger than I would have expected. My abuelo's back is hunched and his gait is broken and shuffling, but his eyes are clear when he asks about his son.

Soledad answers for us, and translates. I thought I would feel awkward, like I didn't belong here with them. And it's true, I don't—I've spent so much of my life pushing this part of me away, out of sight. But despite all that, through the leathery pads of Abuela's fingers, through the loose weave of Abuelo's shirt, something is there, beneath the skin and beyond blood.

My grandparents hold on to Pilar and me and to each other, and tears roll down their creased cheeks. I know those tears. The ones that are half and half. One part joy, to have us here with them, and an equal part sorrow, to know that Papá was left behind.

Late November

nyone looking in from the outside would say my grandparents are terribly poor.

They store all their food in the silo beside the home. What's in there lasts no more than a year. What goes into the silo is no less than every bit of food they were able to coax out of their small plot of land the year before. Quinua, ocas, corn, peppers, potatoes. There is a jar with eight coins on the mantel above the cooking fire. I counted. Eight.

They tell time by the angle of the sun. They gauge the weather by the smell of the air. Abuela has a chicken. Pilar loves that scruffy thing from the second she scatters her first handful of seed. And a goat—they have a goat for milk, too.

Both of my grandparents are missing teeth. Their skin is folded and wrinkled and soft. They look so much older than I remember.

Soledad talks to them. She's teaching Pilar the Aymara language so she can speak to our grandparents on her own. Pilar soaks it up like a cactus about to flower in the rainy season.

Soledad tries with me, too, but the words are like spines on my tongue. She laughs this cackling, uncontrollable laugh when I speak. I don't mind. I think I would do just about anything to hear her laugh.

Soledad is Abuela's shadow. She's different here. So many days of contentment strung together have altered the slopes and rises of her face.

Pilar is Soledad's shadow. She follows behind while they talk about plants and herbs and old stories. She still collects shed snakeskins and dropped feathers, desiccated exoskeletons and snail shells, and gives them as gifts every chance she gets.

The two of them stepped into their first day on the Altiplano like they were stepping into the rest of their lives.

But me? I know this isn't my place. I know I'm going back, and maybe soon. Maybe for a long time. I can't be fully here. Not yet.

Abuela has a *quipu* that tracks the crops and the harvest. It looks like a bunch of knotted cords in different colors all strung in a row. But I can ask (well, Soledad can ask) how much it rained in 1967, and the answer is there, in the knots. She can ask the yield of the quinua crop over the last ten years, and Abuela's fingers drift down the cord to find the answer.

They don't have computers or telephones. They don't have chemicals to test the soil or machines to till the rows. But I'm beginning to wonder if their way, which is the same way it's been done here since before the rule of the Inka, isn't so much better.

Abuelo can't work the soil like Abuela. His lungs won't let him. So he sits on a bench in the shade in front of the house shaping and binding together sets of pan flutes to sell. He does this every day, but I've never heard him play them. I bet his lungs won't let him do that anymore either.

I sit beside him and lean against the wall as he turns a pile of hollow sticks into an instrument. My head drops back. Beyond the thatched roofline, the sky is the kind of blue you only get up here above the haze, above the layers of wispy clouds that hang over the valleys. A blue so clear you'd think you could bend your knees and swan dive into it.

was wrong about this place. And these people. And my place here, with them.

I thought coming to the Altiplano would be taking a giant step backward. I thought anyone who would live up here *was* backward. I didn't think I would see any part of myself here.

Instead, it's like I've taken a giant step to the side. All the crazy energy of the city is still there, spinning out in the valley below us; I'm just taking a break from it for a while. Yeah, the no running water sucks. But my hands don't clench into fists so easily here. They're too busy digging with Abuela in the fields or helping Abuelo milk the goat.

The air is thin. The rhythm of the day is simple. My mind is quiet.

I get it now, when Papá said his poetry came from this place. The Altiplano becomes a part of you, if you let it. It forms like dew on your skin and sinks in through your pores. It alters the chemistry of your blood. It changes you, if you let it.

Soledad and I are suspended in this in-between place, where neither one of us knows what comes next. I know I'd never be able to leave Pilar here without Soledad watching over her. She knows she never would've made it here without me.

But it's more than that. Our lives are stretching out before us, unplanned and unpredictable. Will I even get accepted into university? If I do, how long will I be gone? In a year from now, or two, will this place still feel like home to her?

How often will I be able to visit? And how, now that I know what it feels like to sleep with her in my arms, will I ever be able to leave?

So we don't talk about it. We wake together when the sunlight slants through the open window, we sleep together on an animal-skin mattress, and we make sure we're never far apart in the hours between.

The afternoon heat is punishing. Sweat pours off my skin. Abuelo is sleeping when I duck into the house; his breath sounds like pebbles knocking together. I blink and wait for my eyes to adjust to the darkness inside. Two white rectangles glow faintly from the rug. Envelopes. Somebody must have made the trek to town for the mail.

I float over and kneel down, my skin as thin as the membrane of a helium balloon. I pick up the envelopes and bring them close to my eyes. One is from San Sebastián prison. The other is from the University of San Simón. I weigh the two envelopes in my palms.

How much does a dream weigh? And how much, hope?

I tear open the rectangle with the academic seal and skim down through salutations and introductions.

We are pleased to accept your application to Universidad Mayor de San Simón. This fall, you will be assigned an academic advisor in the law department.

In the dim shack, stars swim in front of my eyes and a sigh as long as the winds carving down the peaks and running the length of the Altiplano leaves my lungs. It's just a beginning, what I'm holding in my hands. But we need this beginning so very badly.

I open the other rectangle with Papá's careful lettering on the front. I unfold the paper. My hands begin to shake.

Francisco,

*Thank you for your letters. You cannot guess
how good it feels to know you and your sister are
safe and to know your grandparents are happy to
have received you.*

*I don't know what I have ever done to deserve
such faithful children. Thank you for taking care of
your sister all this time. Thank you for taking care
of me all this time.*

The page splatters as my heart drains. I turn it over. On the back, through blurry eyes, I see sectioned verses and clumping stanzas flowing like water down the page.

It's a poem.

My father, the poet, has found his words again.

AUTHOR'S NOTE

More than fifteen years ago, I spent a summer during college volunteering in Cochabamba, Bolivia. I worked at a nonprofit facility that provided health care, meals, enrichment opportunities, and a safe place to spend the afternoons for children who lived in the nearby prisons alongside their incarcerated parents.

During my time there, I never met a Francisco, Pilar, or Soledad. These characters are my inventions. I heard stories like theirs, however, and I witnessed their truths in the lives of the young people I worked with. Unfortunately, the tragic effects of the 1008 and the United States' role in both its passage and brutal enforcement are not fictitious.

Bolivia is a constitutional democracy. A law that violated citizens' rights, as the 1008 did, should never have been allowed to stand. Over the years, reforms have amended the law, but not before Bolivia's prisons were overfull and its justice system too bogged down to adequately remedy the damage done to countless families and communities.

In Bolivia, colonialism left behind an intensely stratified society that for centuries oppressed and exploited its indigenous peoples. To complicate matters, Bolivia has long been considered economically to be the poorest country in the region, the effects of which made it vulnerable to foreign intervention.

Today, the country holds the largest proportion of indigenous people on the continent. In recent years, the people of Bolivia have brought about wide-reaching reform to indigenous rights and representation, access to and equity in education, and more. As with any country seeking to create a more just society, however, change takes time, and as of the writing of this book, Bolivia's prison kids are still waiting for justice to find them.

When I left Bolivia and returned to college and my privileged North American life, the human cost of my country's war on drugs weighed heavily on me. The brief time during which I joined those pitting themselves against that particular tangle of crippling poverty, aggressive foreign policy, and persistent injustice has stuck with me.

I'm a writer. When confronted with what seems like an immovable obstacle, the only way I know forward is through story.

Thank you for reading and for sharing this one with me.

GLOSSARY

abuela/abuelo/abuelos: a grandmother/grandfather/
  grandparents

aguayo: a patterned, woven cloth from the Andes region,
  commonly made from llama wool

ají amarillo: a mild chili used to flavor many traditional
  Bolivian dishes

Altiplano: the high plains in the Andes region of Bolivia
  and neighboring countries

anciana: an elderly woman

ayllu: an indigenous community of the Andes region

Aymara: one of the groups of indigenous people of the
  Andes and their language

arroyo: a gully in an arid region that is usually dry except
  after heavy rains

Ballivián, José: a wartime general and the eleventh
  president of Bolivia

biblioteca: a library

boliviano: the currency of Bolivia

bruto: stupid, coarse

campesino: a peasant; the term preferred by many
  to replace the slur "indio" when referring to the
  indigenous peoples of the Andes region

cancha: a large market in Cochabamba

cárcel: a prison

charango: a small guitar-like ten-stringed instrument

cholita: a Bolivian woman who dresses in traditional indigenous clothing (Her attire indicates not only whether she is Quechua, Aymara, or a member of one of the other indigenous nations, but also which region of the country she is from.)

chu'lo: a knitted wool hat with earflaps

chuño: a dehydrated potato with a very long shelf life, a staple of the Andean diet

cobarde: a coward

coca: a bush commonly grown throughout the Andes with leaves that can be processed to produce cocaine but that, in their natural form, act merely as a mild stimulant comparable to coffee

cocada: a coconut cookie

cojudo: profanity; in Bolivia, an asshole

Cordilleras: parallel mountain ranges in the Andes

Día de los Muertos: the Day of the Dead

escabeche de verduras: pickled vegetables

fútbol: soccer

futbolito: a version of soccer played in small spaces

gato montés: a wild cat native to the Andes

gringo: in Spanish-speaking countries and contexts, citizens of the United States; particularly white people

hacienda: a landed estate

hacendados: people who own haciendas

indio/india: a slur used to label an indigenous man/woman

Inka: the largest empire in pre-Columbian America

ley: a law

mestizo: a person of mixed European and indigenous descent

oca: an edible South American tuber

Oficina de Tránsito: the division of police responsible for traffic and highways

Pachamama: Mother Earth; a goddess in Andean religious traditions

pan con queso: a cheese-covered bun or other variation commonly served for breakfast

picante de pollo: a traditional dish consisting of a spiced sauce and chicken, and served with rice or chuño

profesor/profesora: a male/female teacher

pucha: interjection; in Bolivia, an exclamation of surprise, frustration, or exasperation

puya: a bromeliad native to South and Central America

Quechua: one of the groups of indigenous people of the Andes and their language

quinua: a grain native to the Andes, internationally known as quinoa

quipu: a series of colored, knotted strings hung from a principal strand and used for counting and record-keeping in the Inka empire

salteña: a Bolivian savory pastry filled with meat, sauce, and vegetables

serenata: a serenade

singani: a type of spirits produced in Bolivia

sopa de maní: a soup made from peanuts and potatoes

tantawawa: a sweet bread baked to celebrate the Day of the Dead

Todos Santos: All Saints' Day

trancapecho: a steak sandwich

ven: come

vicuña: a wild animal related to the llama that lives in the high alpine areas of the Andes

wawitay: a term of endearment

SELECTED SOURCES

Allen, Catherine J. *The Hold Life Has: Coca and Cultural Identity in an Andean Community.* Washington, D.C.: Smithsonian Institution Press, 2002. Print.

Kohl, Benjamin H. and Linda Farthing, with Poma F. F. Muruchi. *From the Mines to the Streets: A Bolivian Activist's Life.* Austin: University of Texas Press, 2011. Print.

Ritter, Martha, ed. *Children of Law 1008.* Cochabamba, Bolivia: Andean Information Network, 1996. Print.

Steele, Liza and Edward Telles. "Pigmentocracy in the Americas: How is Educational Attainment Related to Skin Color?" *AmericasBarometer Insights: 2012,* Number 73. PDF file.

Youngers, Coletta, and Eileen Rosin, eds. *Drugs and Democracy in Latin America: The Impact of U.S. Policy.* Boulder, Colo.: L. Rienner, 2005. Print.

ACKNOWLEDGMENTS

No matter how much research an author undertakes, there are nuances only an expert can understand. I am indebted to the following people for sharing their conversation, abundant knowledge, insight, and fierce love for the country and people of Bolivia with me: Flora Teran, Dr. Juan Carlos Madeni, Pamela Lagrava de Madeni, Anthony Choque, Dr. Carol Conzelman, Marcela Olivera and Lee Cridland. Any outstanding errors or omissions are my own.

Thank you to my brilliant editor, Liza Kaplan, who champions her projects with enthusiasm and absolute commitment. Thank you to the wonderful people at Philomel, and to the greater Penguin team that has worked so expertly to put this book into the hands of readers: Michael Green, Talia Benamy, Maria Fazio, Jenny Chung, David Briggs, Emily Rodriguez, Liz Lunn, Ana Deboo, Kathleen Keating, and Bridget Hartzler.

Thanks, as always, to my agent, Ammi-Joan Paquette. For their keen eyes and kind critique, I am grateful to my early readers: Lisa Schroeder, Kristin Derwich, Meg Wiviott, Laura Resau and Tiffany Crowder.

Finally, I could not do this work without the love and support of my wife. Truly, I'm the lucky one.

Read an excerpt from Melanie Crowder's
critically acclaimed novel

AUDACITY

clouds

Over the gray plain of the sea
winds are gathering the storm-clouds

Words
float like wayward clouds
in the air
in my mind.

Now his wing the wave

       Wait—
or was it,

Now the wave his wing caresses

I dip a hand
into my apron pocket
unfold a square of paper
against my palm,
hunch my shoulder,
hide it from view.

       Ah,

yes.

Now his wing the wave caresses,
now he rises like an arrow
cleaving clouds
and

The poem is ripped
from my hand
and the air,

where only wayward clouds
had been,
is full of shouting,
accusations
a hand raised in anger
        ready to strike—

                the world slows
        in the second before
        pain blooms
        in my jaw;
            a second
        to hope
        the poem is
                        safe
in my mind
where fists
    and fury
cannot shake it free.

ordinary

Just because I am
small-boned
and short,
brown-haired
and brown-eyed,
just because I look

common
as a wren
meek
as a robin

that does not mean
what is inside me is also

common
as a wren
meek
as a robin.

Everything
I wish for
is strange
aberrant
even wrong in this place
but I know
I cannot be the only one
blanketing her bright feathers
hooding her sharp eyes
hiding
in plain sight.

My life
　　　　so far

has been ordinary
simple
small

but I cannot shake the feeling
that inside this little body
something stronger
is nesting
waiting
for a chance
to flex her talons
snap her wings
         taut
and glide
far away
from here.